64110

NELLIE CAMERON

◊⊱

NELLIE CAMERON

❀❀❀❀❀❀❀❀❀❀❀❀❀❀❀❀❀❀❀❀❀❀❀❀❀❀❀❀❀❀❀❀❀❀❀

by Michele Murray

DRAWINGS BY LEONORA E. PRINCE

THE SEABURY PRESS
NEW YORK

*to my Mother
and in memory of my Grandmother*

chapter 1

EVERY SUNDAY Nellie went to Zion African Methodist Episcopal Church just down the long sloping block from her house. Today was no different. Down the strangely silent streets they went and into the tall stone building with its own fence and grass, and into the dark place. They all sat in one row on the shiny wooden seats— Mama, then Nellie, who had been nine for only one month; then Sam, who was twelve; then Grace, who was almost fourteen; then Ramona, who was sixteen; then Jesse last of all. He was the baby, only four years old. Willie never came. He was twenty-one, big enough to stay out Saturday night and sleep on Sunday. Daddy was driving his cab.

So it was just the six of them, Nellie closest to Mama.

She had been scared long ago, scared of the organ and the preacher and the deep noises as the church filled up with people. Even their friends looked different on Sunday all dressed up. Now she was bigger and part of the Sundays, and it was like home, a place as close as your own skin.

Nellie closed her eyes and heard Mama's flowery dress rustle. Mama smelled of soapsuds and starch and sweet hair cream.

Sam sat next to Nellie, not singing, not praying, his hands clenched together and his whole face turning down. Nellie knew he was sitting next to her; she could reach out and touch the knee of his shiny best suit. But he wasn't really there, not his eyes, not his thinking. Where was he? Nellie didn't know.

Mama looked at him and sighed and squeezed Nellie's hand.

Ramona kept a good sharp eye on that Jesse. Ramona was a lot like Mama, big and quiet. Now that she was old enough, she was talking about leaving school and going to work. She was practicing on Jesse and Nellie so she could get a good job watching children. Mama and Daddy said there was no such job and she should stay in school, but Ramona was too big to listen to them.

Last night she had stood up at the supper table when Mama started on her again. "Mama, you had your life, whyn't you let me have mine? So I won't get anyplace. What do you know about getting anyplace yourself?

Working and churching, that's what you know! And you plan to tell me *anything?*"

Ramona hadn't even shouted. That would have been better. She spoke low and hard, as if she had thought out each word and polished it before it left her mouth.

Daddy went to slap her but Mama shook her head, saying nothing, just sitting and spooning food into her mouth. Ramona slammed the door into the bedroom. Sam, Jesse, and Nellie looked at each other, then at Mama and Daddy. Mama said, "You want some more food? Well, speak up, then."

Although no one had asked one single question, after a while Mama said, as if answering, "Maybe she right."

And that was all.

Now Ramona was in church with them, as if nothing had happened.

In the lingering summer of September the old church was mighty hot, even with the big windows open all the way. People kept fanning and white hankies were flying and all the fat ladies like Mama sighed and sweated, but Preacher Evans kept on all the same, hot or cold. Sometimes sun shone through the windows; today it danced like a lot of butterflies on the stone wall behind the altar.

Outside, cars and buses went past, not caring about Preacher Evans or the singing or Sunday morning. Still, the day was different. Nellie liked standing up and hollering out the words about Jesus and heaven and precious Lord. She liked the sound of Mama's deep singing coming up out of her and hitting the church roof. Sweat was dripping down Mama's face and she squashed Nellie's hand good and tight.

Preacher Evans now, he used too many words in Nellie's mind. They rolled on by like a river. Grace looked at her and she rolled her eyes back at Grace. Oh my, that man could talk! Mama sat with a sweet smile on her lips and her eyes closed. This was the only time of the entire week Mama's hands lay folded in her lap.

Nellie's feet fell asleep and she kicked against the wooden pew to wake them up. Sam turned to give her a sulky look. "Can't you even behave *decently?*" he whispered sharply.

"Look who's talking!" Nellie whispered back. "Huh!" She kicked again. Her feet thunked against the wood. Sam reached down and grabbed hold of her ankles and held them still. "Stop it!" Ramona *sssh'd* them from all the way down the row. Mama still smiled.

Nellie heard *paradise* and liked that sound. Para-dise. Para-dose. Para-dese. She tried out the sounds in her head and they all sounded good. She wondered how they looked printed out like in her schoolbooks and then she got a creepy feeling in her stomach. Why did she bring *that* to mind? Crummy books. She couldn't read them. And she didn't want to. Stupid books.

She tugged hard at Mama's hand. Mama frowned and pulled away. Nellie squnched around on the bench and scratched her head. Mama frowned again and whispered into her ear, "Hush now!" Then Mama straightened up and shouted, "Amen! Amen! Say it, that's surely the way it is!"

All around them other people were shouting, "Amen! Amen! Glory! Glory!" That meant the end of the service was upon them. Only Sam did not shout one single word. He looked up at the church ceiling and kept his lips locked tight together.

Mama made them wait until the church was almost empty before they could file out. Grace and Ramona raced down the block to talk to some friends. Mama watched with her lips pursed when she saw that there were boys joining the group. "Sam, go after your sisters," she said. "Go on now, don't slouch. You like to double up soon you keep on that way."

"Ah, Mama, please . . ." Sam looked straight into Mama's eyes. "I don't like those kids."

"No," said Mama. "Neither I. Oh, you understand, child! Now, go on, look out!"

Sam waited a moment, then slouched down the street. Mama's sigh went right down to her toes. She talked quietly to Sister Stone and Brother Williams about Preacher Evans's sermon. "He surely do uplift my heart," Mama said.

"He speak with angels' tongues," Sister Stone said, nodding. The three red feathers on top of her pale gray hat looked as if they would come off with each nod, but they only flopped this way and that and finally came back to where they started, right on top of the hat.

"God's voice," said Brother Williams in his deep grave way. He was Nellie's godfather, an old friend of Daddy's from South Carolina. Nellie couldn't remember when he wasn't a guest in their house at least once a week, his long legs stretched out as he sat and talked. It was Brother Williams who had written and told Daddy that life was better in Washington and why didn't he and Mama come up, too, and make a new life.

Now Brother Williams was talking about the sermon and Mama was agreeing and holding tight to Jesse's hand while Jesse jumped around. Nellie slid up close to Mama, just plain waiting.

"Miss Nellie, and how are you this glorious morning of the Lord's day?" Brother Williams rubbed the top of her head with his big hand. Nellie looked up as high as his tie, and then right past him to see Emma Rice standing on the corner.

"Fine," Nellie said, and ran. "Emma, Emma, wait on me!"

"I'm going nowhere fast," Emma called back. "Look like Gran'll be talking here all day."

"Where you been this summer, huh? Oh, Emma, I called you when I had my birthday, and you never answered the phone, not even once." Nellie looked at her reproachfully.

All last year Emma and Nellie had been best friends. Emma had lived right around the corner with her Gran, a cook at Sea Island Style, and no one else in her family at all. Just the two of them. Then the terrible thing happened—Sea Island Style moved across town. And so did Gran. And Emma with her.

"Emma, how I missed you!" Nellie said sadly.

Emma smiled at her in that lazy way she had. "I been sick," she said briefly. "Gran sent me back home. I wanted to call, Nell, really I did, then I forgot." Emma shuddered in the heat. "I hated it back home . . . my Daddy, he's got himself another wife, you see . . . she thought I was uppity, she said so." Emma's low voice was flat. "I didn't feel like writing, you know, Nell."

"Emma, can you come and see me?"

"I'll call you right soon, I'll call you."

"Promise?"

"Oh, Nell, you are the funniest thing! Whyever not?"

"Emma, remember when I came to see you, remember? Maybe Mama'll carry me on up again soon. When she not so busy."

"Gran don't like no mess a-tall," Emma said in her flat voice again. Then she smiled. "We sure did have a good time, though."

Jesse called in his shrill voice, "Hey, Nell, where you been? Come on now, Mama on her way!"

Nellie and Emma clasped hands.

"Promise?"

"Promise."

"You been talking," Jesse said when Nellie came running back to them, "you been talking just like Mama 'n Grace 'n Ramona. Ain't no one talking to me."

The air was going out of Sunday as far as Nellie was concerned. How slowly they walked! The street was full of people strolling slowly up and down. All the women wore bright dresses and big hats in pink and red and blue and green and yellow and white and purple and orange. The street looked like a moving flower garden! The men sweated inside their heavy black suits.

Even though it was Sunday, lots of shops were still open. The laundromat was always open. Slim the Barber was all lit up, with men sitting in the chairs and the radio blaring away. People were going in and out of the drugstore. Then Mama found a dollar bill in her purse and they stopped by the bakery to buy hot rolls.

"Sunday treat, my lambs," Mama said, letting them smell the good smell of those rolls as they walked on down the street to their place.

"I do hope that lazy Willie be up with the coffee on," Ramona grumbled.

Mama hushed her. "He work hard all week, the Lord knows he has a good heart."

Sam burst out laughing. "Where he be until so late last night then? Man, he rolled up the night before he stopped!"

Mama turned on him. "How you know that? You been up reading in bed again with the flashlight?" Oh, she was mad! Good thing Mama didn't slap on Sundays. Sam skipped out of her way anyhow.

"Willie got himself a girl friend," Grace said, giggling. "He don't think anyone know about it, but I know. Just happen he pick a girl, she's got a sister in my class."

Mama winked at Grace. "Happen *I* know, too—so now we all got a secret!"

Finally they got to their corner. Nellie thought their place was bright and sunny, especially after their old house, which had been falling down all around them. Mama didn't mind cleaning and Daddy didn't mind fixing, but when the rats came around and the rent went up, Daddy said, "Paying for six chil'rens 'n us is fine but I don't aim to pay for no rats besides." Nellie remembered the old house only a little; they had left it two years before and had never gone back to the old neighborhood way at the other end of the city, far from everything.

Now they were close to downtown and the buses Mama had to take to get to her cleaning jobs. If you took the bus right at their corner and just kept going downtown on it, you'd be at the Washington Monument. Mama had taken Nellie and Jesse once but they didn't go up all that long way to the top. Jesse had been too scared.

Their new place had no more rats, and when Mama finished fixing the rooms, they looked downright beautiful. They had a front room which Mama called the parlor but the rest of them called the living room, a kitchen with enough room for their dining table, and four small and dark bedrooms.

A shoemaker had his shop downstairs. They went up the stairs in the hallway next to his store and they were at their own door. The front room was the best, with the flowered rug Willie bought last Christmas with his job money. Right by the window was the table with more flowers on the shiny cloth.

Only time Mama said anything nice about the South was when she talked about the flowers growing in their yard long ago. She said their names soft and low, then looked out the window at the street, and shook her head. For Nellie the street was the best play place of all and the printed flowers were just fine. The South was only a story.

Willie was in his bathrobe at the table, and the coffee was perking away with soft little puffs. The smell of coffee made the room feel rich.

"Morning, son," Mama said, leaning over to kiss Willie. "Look at that mustache, now, will you?"

Willie patted down the thin hair growing above his lip. "Like it, Mama?"

Mama studied him. "Well, son, you just growing up awful fast on me is all."

"You look like a real dude, Willie," Ramona said, smiling.

"Some fancy dude!" Sam suddenly broke in. His voice was harsh, almost strangling in his throat. "Oh, man, you really have it!"

Willie jumped right up out of his chair, knocking the

chair over. "Shut your mouth, kid!" he shouted. "What do you know?"

"Huh!" Grace snorted. "Someone in this family think he know *everything!*" And she made a face at Sam.

Mama was shaking. "On Sunday! Can't you chil'rens ever stop?" She sank down into a chair and wiped her eyes.

Very quiet now, Ramona and Grace hurried about putting food on the table. They spread the margarine and jelly thin to fill the whole dozen rolls, then Mama came up with some cheese and graham crackers to add to the stuff on the table. Nellie had some of yesterday's cornbread cold and thought it was the best of all. Mama had made it.

Jesse wanted to take his roll down on the floor where his battered old truck was and Mama said *yes* after a while of his begging. Being the baby, Jesse got a lot of things his way. Not Nellie.

Mama was reading her Bible and listening for Daddy. Nellie watched her finger moving along from line to line keeping the place. Willie was all folded up in the newspaper. His long fingers were rappeting and tappeting on the table, making a dance, sounding like the drummer at the Booker T. Music Hall. Ramona was practicing on them all again, making oatmeal, which Nellie really didn't hate. But she made believe she did each day. Why? Maybe the sour look on Ramona's face. That Ramona! Who voted her boss-lady?

Sam had one comic section and Grace had the other, and they were getting in each other's way and kicking. Mama said, "Plenty of time for spankings on Monday!"

"Hey, want me to read you the comics?" Sam asked. He sounded sweet as soda pop, but Nellie knew he was just being mean, reminding her. Like Ramona wanting to tie her shoes way back when she was in first grade!

"Don't care about your crummy old comics, anyway," she mumbled. "Mama, can I watch the TV?"

"Girl, what you say? No, ma'am. Not on the Lord's day."

They hadn't heard Daddy come in, after all, but there he was in the doorway. "Never mind no Lord's day, Minnie," he told Mama. "It's Eli Cameron's day, that's for sure, and he done had more than enough of the TV noise all week."

From the way he twinkled, Nellie knew Daddy had had a good morning bringing old ladies to and from church. He walked slow and easy to the table, poured himself some coffee and ate a roll before he said another word. "Guess I can figure up on the Lord's day, Minnie, eh?"

With a pencil stub he calculated on the edge of the newspaper, then took out his bills and change and divided them into three piles. One belonged to the cab company. That went in a brown envelope. One was for Daddy after the cab company man noted it down in his own book. Nellie watched the third pile closely. That was the tips, all for Daddy alone. Mama watched, too.

Daddy pulled two dimes from his pocket and added them to the pile. "Four dollars even with those thrown in," he said slowly.

They were all saving for a Ray Charles album. A quarter went into the old can with a slit in it. Willie threw in a dime. Then Ramona added a quarter of her own baby-sitting money. Mama counted it again. "Almost two dollars. Looks like next week we can make it, maybe." That was something to think about! Nellie was excited already.

Daddy got a dollar for tobacco money. Ramona got her regular three quarters. Grace needed fifty cents for one small thing and another and Sam did, too. Mama looked at that last dollar for a long time, then she took out a quarter for carfare to her cleaning job the next day.

"Know what, Minnie?" Daddy said. "Better hand over fifty cents for my insurance." The insurance was one thing Daddy was serious about. "More I put in, more to come out for you, Minnie, and the chil'rens besides."

Mama reached over the table and put her big dark hand on top of Daddy's bony lighter one. "You right, Eli, thinking that way. Well, look what's left now!" She pointed to the dime and nickel on the table and laughed. "Pretty skinny if you ask me!"

Nellie could hardly breathe.

"Nell, go get me your jar," Mama said, and in went the dime and the nickel. Same as always. "When you can read me one book now . . ." Nellie never got any other money unless she took bottles back for Mrs. Dempster who lived above them on the third floor.

In the dark bedroom Nellie almost cried. She pushed the jar back under her clothes in her own drawer. It was heavy and almost full; she must have a hundred dollars in that dumb jar now. Why, with all that money you didn't have to know how to read! You just went around pointing and someone else told you all you had to know. She'd hire Sam to do her reading for her if only he wouldn't tease her from morning to night. Sometimes she wished Sam would just talk to her but he never had any time. No more did all the others.

She would show them! Oh, she would surprise the lot of them one fine day! Then they would have time for her. A million hours or so . . . they'd forget all about that Sam. He would just beg to talk to her and she . . . she'd turn her head away and . . .

She had no idea. Just nothing, she guessed. Nothing she could do to make anyone notice her, stuck away in the middle like that, only one more girl.

So she took out her paper doll, Francina, and played a story of a country world, black fields and blue hot sky, like in Mama's talking of South Carolina. There was no school at all to worry about, only the smell of the fields, the flowers, and the mules.

For once the room was quiet. Ramona slept in the top bunk and Grace in the bottom one. Nellie had a folding cot only opened up at night because you couldn't walk otherwise. They each had one drawer in the dresser and a mirror to share. Hardly ever was Nellie alone as she was now.

In the front room Mama and Daddy talked and stopped, then talked again. She heard Willie go out, then Ramona, and Mama saying, "You watch out now, girl," and "Let her just be, Eli, she a good girl."

Grace called, "Nellie! Nellie!" but she would not answer. She heard the sound of Grace's ball and jacks on the floor. If she had answered, she would be playing with Grace now. She heard Sam slam the door of his room. "I wish this whole world would burn," she whispered. This feeling crept up on her from time to time. She could do nothing about it.

A long time ago, it seemed, she had seen the world burning on the TV, the beautiful flames pulled upward by the wind and the crisp sounds of fire coming right out of the TV itself. Men were running around. Some were putting out the fires. Some were grabbing things from the burning stores and running.

Nellie had been scared. But it wasn't the fires scared her so much as the kind of great joy she felt at watching all that burning. Suppose it really happened, she thought, and not only on TV, but right here in real life, the way it had been in those other places?

Nellie's mouth went dry and she felt too worn out to move. She thought this was how a grave would be, so cold and heavy and alone. She didn't know what she wanted but she knew that no one had ever given it to her. Something wonderful. What?

She had a glimpse of it in the pages of those books she hated and would not read because they laughed at her with something she could never have. She had said *no* to that world even while she sat in her seat all smiling and quiet, playing a game of learning. Now she was just plain dumb, no matter how you dressed it up. And the world might as well burn down, as far as she cared.

Jesse came crawling in after his truck. "Nellie, hey, Nellie, what you be doing in here? Play with me. I let you be the truck driver if you do."

Then she really started in with that hateful crying she could not stop. "Don't go, Jesse," she whispered. "Stay on here with me."

But he followed his truck right out of the room again and into the kitchen. Seemed like they were all going away from her and she was left alone in the dark, quiet room, being no one very much. Paradise seemed like a far place away, beyond South Carolina and the endless fields her Mama hated so.

chapter 2

❀❀❀❀❀❀❀❀❀❀❀❀❀❀❀❀❀❀

NOW THAT SEPTEMBER was well underway, every Monday meant the start of another week of school. Sundays were just beautiful when you compared. Nellie never wanted to let go of Sundays, no matter what. But there was Monday morning like a slap at the beginning of the week, harder than ever to bear after the lazy, sweet summer habits.

Mama was shaking them and Nellie had to rush and fold up that old cot so Ramona and Grace could get on out of their bunks. And then she was only in the way. So she hunched up in Grace's bed back in the corner by the wall all covered up with blankets and watched her sisters running around. Ramona was quick and quiet, braiding her hair and fixing her blouse and skirt as if they were really nice clothes and she proud to be wearing them. Grace lazed here and there, falling on the bed and giggling. She was reading while she dressed.

Ramona shoved her. "Your turn to make lunches, Gracie. Why you waste your time reading that stuff? You got some mighty crazy ideas, know that? Boy oh man, you look one holy mess. Mama won't like it."

"Mind your own business," Grace said absently. She never paid Ramona any mind but went on reading, untangling her hair without looking. "Hey, Nellie, remember that story I told you? I found it again in this book." She bent over the pages, smiling to herself.

Nellie closed her eyes and thought of the princess in the deep woods and the lost feeling she had and the small house and the witch and the prince. In some ways it was jumbled up in her mind but was very clear in others.

The unwelcoming morning disappeared and she felt a warm green breeze on her face. A blue sky. No gray light from the window where you could see nothing but a brick wall. Oh, how she would like to go into that small house in the woods and sit on the painted chair and be near the fire! Maybe Grace would tell her the story again if she took care of Jesse some afternoon.

Then Mama was shaking her again. "Nellie Cameron! You get on up and out! I mean, you are worse than that Jesse! You are not the baby anymore, missy!" And it was all a rush. Getting dressed. Eating her oatmeal cold while Sam glared at her. Ramona already off to high school and Grace on the way to the junior high that was falling apart day by day. Willie was gulping and running and Daddy halfway out the door still chewing and Mama rushing around with her hat on and a cup of coffee in her hand.

"C'mon, slowpoke," Sam growled.

"Why you in such a hurry to get to that place, anyway?" Nellie asked. "Old jail." Sam was hustling Jesse into his coat.

"Now, Nell, you wash up these dishes when you get home, hear now?" Mama said. "Then you can go out and play when Grace comes in to watch Jesse. Ramona'll get the supper started." She stood looking to see if she had forgotten anything. Then she went on out and the house seemed empty all at once, even though four of them were still sitting and drinking their cocoa. That was Mama.

Nellie grumbled all the way to school. "What a way for a day to start! Don't even leave the skin on a person!"

She and Sam dropped Jesse off at his sitter's house. He cried same as every day. They never told Mama. There was no good to it. There was no good to anything. Especially not school. Nellie grumbled and mumbled.

Sam listened to just so much, but he had his troubles, too, which he never shared with anyone. "Well, shoot, girl, you got to grow up and do something some day. Where's your pride? Me, I aim to be something really fine, something big. But you, you just going to end up cleaning other people's houses, like Mama." His words were not harsh but firm, as if he had thought it all out for himself and knew where he was going.

Mama was good enough for Nellie. Sam scared her, to tell the truth. Mama managed fine with her Bible and her Dream Book. Everything you had to know for living was in the Bible, Mama said, and the Dream Book told you what every kind of dream meant. She could even tell if someone's coming baby would be a boy or a girl just from the dreams they had!

Sam made fun of the Dream Book, but Nellie loved it with its shiny red cover and gold lettering. Oh, if she could only get her nose inside that book and make some sense out of it! If her teacher, Mrs. Grady, gave them a book like that, why Nellie knew she'd read it in a snap. As usual, when she thought of it, reading was easy.

Then in the middle of her dreams the school stood above her and she knew it was no good. No dreams could make that old school go away. It was too big, all dirty and gray with broken windows and a high fence. Here she was in third grade and could not even open the heavy school doors. Dumb fat doors. About a dozen boys had to push against them before they creaked slowly open. "Who'd they build this place for, anyway? Giants?"

But Sam was off to the boys' yard. Nellie put a smile on her face and went around the corner to the girls' yard, part of her really happy and part playing a game.

Still and all, the yard was not the bad part. Nellie could have stayed there in the yard all day with her friends LaVerne, Susy, and Orinda. Even the girls in the "fast" third grade admired her rope jumping, and she could beat them at jacks. And she knew more games than almost anyone because Grace and Ramona had taught them to her. So she smiled without pretending and her pigtails bounced against the collar of her blouse as she jumped in the best corner of the girls' yard, beating out Lissa Goff, who was in fifth grade. Without warning she felt good, inside and out.

True, she still missed Emma; seeing her again yesterday made Nellie miss her even more today. All last year they had hung around together, proud that they had been friends. Emma was the best student. Nellie was the best at games. Once Emma said she wished she could tell jokes and jump rope like Nellie. Emma was quiet and kind of fat. No one else in the entire class knew as much as she did, but in the yard she had just stood and watched until Nellie came along. So they fitted together real well. And Emma never said one single word about Nellie being dumb.

"Morning, Nellie!"

"Orinda, how you doing?"

"See the TV Saturday night? See that crazy show? Man, my Momma said she have nightmares thinking about those creatures!"

"Jesse, he scared. Not me, though."

Orinda ducked away. Toby Flite was after her, jamming his hand against her shoulder.

Nellie felt a push, too. "Watch yourself there, Joe Lee!"

"Yah, yah, don't have to. Make me, make me!"

But he was all bluff and scare. Nellie paid no attention to him.

A whistle called the boys back to their own yard.

"Got your jacks?" LaVerne asked.

LaVerne Cooper was Nellie's best friend this year. She held out her jacks and ball in the palm of her hand. She was wearing a purple velvet coat far too big for her, probably her Ma's old man-getting coat. All the buttons were off. It was pinned with two big safety pins, but through the big gaps Nellie could see LaVerne's ragged dress. There was a big tear down one side; Nellie was sure that was why she was wearing the coat to school.

Nellie pulled her jacks and ball out of her pocket and they got down to serious play at once.

LaVerne threw the ball and missed. "Don't know what's getting into this old self today."

"Getting sick? I just had the flu."

"Don't know. Maybe. So what? My Ma'll never do a thing for it. She don't care." LaVerne tossed the jack ball into the air. "All last night she was fighting—oooh, you should have *heard* her! My sister Anna, she never said one word back. But this morning she just moved on out with the baby an' all. I'm gonna miss that Butchie baby, I think. And my Ma said she didn't care one bit. She said once I be big enough to work, I could get out, too, then she would be happy for once."

"You going to?" Nellie asked. They had fights in her house, sure, but her Mama would never say such words to any of them. Never. Oh, she had heard stories like LaVerne's, but always, far away, somehow safe.

LaVerne leaned over to tie her old sneakers. "I tell you something, Nell, I'm not going to grow up. I just going to stay in the third grade forever and then my Ma, why, she'll have to take care of me."

Nellie stared at her friend. "I'm scairt they going to *leave* me back—my Mama and my Daddy both, they'd whup me for that, sure. Why you want to stay back there? Oooh, LaVerne, don't say that! Some day I'm going to be big, like Ramona, and smart, like Sam, and then all of them will have to pay attention to me. I'm going to get me a good job," she said dreamily, "and buy Mama something real nice. A fur coat. That's it. Soft and nice . . ."

"Hey, you think they going to leave you back?" La-Verne asked in a different voice.

Nellie felt sick. "Oh, no! I been trying. It's only early in the year. You'll see, I'm going to do real good."

"Not me," LaVerne said proudly. "My Ma don't care. Only the kids'll all laugh. . . . I'll kill them!"

Nellie bragged. "I'm learning to read now. Real good.

You'll see. I'm surprising *everyone!*"

She threw the jacks and caught almost all of them. Then the ball bounced away and she ran to get it. Leroy Clagget pulled her pigtails and she chased him around. "Dumb, dumb, dumb!" he called after her. She threw the ball right at his head and bopped him one but good. "I am not dumb!"

Leroy turned around and stuck out his tongue at her. "That's not what I hear from Sam," he shouted. "He says you the dumbest thing on two legs." Then he threw her ball back right into her face and ran off.

Nellie just stood there, absolutely still and silent. She knew how La Verne felt with her awful mother. She felt nothing at all. Only a big hole where something should have been. Had Sam really said that about her, her Sam? She didn't believe it, not even in the first flush of hate that sickened her. He was strange and hard to himself and everyone else, but he wasn't cruel. Only—why was it cruel? It was true.

She threw the ball back to LaVerne. "You keep all the jacks today. I'm going to swing!" Run, run, run. Her feet pounded on the concrete. Run, run, run. The world was blurred if you kept on running fast enough.

Not even the older girls could swing as high and as far as Nellie. Her pigtails swept out behind her as she stood up and swung back and forth over the yard. High, high, high. Fast, fast, fast. She pumped furiously, then felt the release of the rhythm bellying her out. Like a bird she floated lightly on the air.

Suppose she fell. She had never thought of that. Then they would all be sorry they had made fun of her. She looked way down at that hard concrete and decided she wouldn't fall. She even decided she wouldn't be scared, and she swung out higher than she ever had before, keeping her eyes fixed right on the gray sky. If only she could keep on going!

Nothing could drive the words out of her mind, though. Only one way to handle them, and she knew it. She could read some words, after all. She had only to put them together with the words she couldn't read, then learn those words, too, and that would be that. She wished with all her heart to be as smart as Sam was. She would make him eat his crazy words!

The bell rang from far inside the building, then stopped, then rang again. Three times. The kids began to move toward the doors, dragging their feet.

Nellie swung up and down real high once more, then slowed down. Slower and slower, lower and lower, until she jumped off near the ground and ran to get her books. She just made it. She liked to cut the lines as thin as she could between being on time and too late.

She told herself that she would change right from this very minute. "You dumb yourself," she hissed at Leroy as he ran past to get into the boys' line. She stood waiting to go on, seeing herself with a thick book, reading without even moving her lips the way Sam did. Mama school. Hear? Keep yourself where you belongs, right in here!" Mama tapped Nellie's head, then her chest. "Sam, he don't know," Mama said grimly. "He gots to learn by hisself. Specially around white folks think they know *everything!* Why, they don't know nothing, nothing that counts."

"Yes'm. Only, Mama—Miz Webster ain't white, nor Mr. Truesdale neither."

"There's black folks even worse'n white, 'cause they playing white and they purely ain't." Mama clasped Nellie's hands inside her own big ones, closed her eyes, and kissed Nellie right smack on her nose.

Now walking into school Nellie wrinkled her nose and felt Mama's kiss again. She would do what Mama said, behave herself, and learn the magic tricks of reading.

chapter 3

IT COULDN'T LAST. Who'd expect it to? For a start, Mrs. Grady called her "Ellen." Nellie knew very well her birth name was Ellen. Why didn't Mrs. Grady know that her usual name was just Nellie? Since Mrs. Grady insisted on "Ellen," Nellie acted as if she had never heard of any Ellen Cameron and looked at the floor when Mrs. Grady spoke to this Ellen-girl.

Mrs. Grady grew still and sharp. She talked entirely too much about manners and respect and good behavior, finishing off by threats to call Mama to school. But all of this had to do with a girl named Ellen, not Nellie.

Mainly Nellie sat at her desk and tuned Mrs. Grady in and out, like some transistor radio. She hated the room with its peeling green paint, ripped shades, and dirty windows. Cardboard patches covered holes where two panes had been broken. A few old ripped maps, dusty and curling up at the edges, decorated the walls. The overhead lights shed a glare in some places and left other spots in half-shadow. Mrs. Grady's begonia was dying.

Nellie sighed and opened her books. The big windows in the room reflected the sun like a burning glass, making it sparkle in long rays on the walls and board. Sometimes Nellie couldn't see anything but bright dazzle against her eyes. Today the sun was low but fierce and the heat burned through her thin dress. At the same time her feet in their sneakers were cold against the old damp wooden floor.

Mrs. Grady had told her not to wear sneakers—or else! Mama had to come all the way up to school and lose two hours' pay to tell Mrs. Grady that Nellie had no shoes until Grace got new ones. Then Nellie could wear Grace's, which were nice red penny loafers. Grace took care of them.

Mama had looked strained on the way to school but they didn't talk about it between them, not then, not after. Nellie knew Mama hated Mrs. Grady, too, but that she could do nothing about her. Nothing at all. And since Nellie couldn't read, she was stuck in this class with all the other dumb ones.

When she had started school, Nellie was certain reading would be easy. Sam could read real well, Grace could read, even Ramona, who hated school, could read some. But she still got sick when she remembered her first grade teacher, Miss Taylor. Every time you made even a tiny mistake, she made you feel too dumb to live. And more. She made you feel you didn't even deserve to learn to read. She kept talking about how lucky they all were to have such lovely books to read and lovely paints and paper and pencils. She thought everything was lovely but the children. They were bad.

Nellie never said a word at home. Just like with Mrs. Grady, what good would it do? Daddy said they were getting an education, more than he had got. That's why they had come up to the city, for the kids to get an education. Now here it was. Nellie said, "Yes, sir."

Mama tried to help her but Mama didn't read too well herself. "You got to do better, girl," was all she said, finally. "You got to apply yourself. You can make it."

They kept promoting her at school, always telling her she was dumb and keeping her with the dumb kids. Nellie didn't think she was dumb. Not smart like Sam. OK. But not dumb. She did her numbers pretty well. But reading was like a mountain she would never cross. She could see the top and it was beautiful, but she had no idea how to get up there.

Today Nellie looked at the page open in front of her and saw a picture of a large white house with trees all around. Across the page some children were running toward the porch. There was a dog chasing them and a cat in a tree. Way back in the picture their parents stepped out of a car a zillion years old. Nellie thought, why I can draw better any old day. She sighed again.

For one thing the book was falling apart. Two pages were gone already and the back cover was bent. For another Mrs. Grady was rapping on the desk and calling for complete attention for the fiftieth time, and the noise of the teacher, added to the noise of the class, gave her a headache. She looked down at the words. Stupid old book. "Jane is happy," it said. Nellie looked down again at the running girl. Is Jane happy? No. From the look on her face she had to go to the bathroom. That was probably why she was running back to the house so fast. Nellie giggled behind her hand.

Anyway, she could read this book, at least some of it. It was a second-grade reader. In readers she was fine. She thought she had read every single first-grade and second-grade reader ever made.

Mrs. Grady said, "Mona's group—write the answers to the questions on this sheet. Frank's group—do the arithmetic problems on page 49—and no talking about them while you're working! Charlene's group—let me see."

Nellie was in Charlene's group. What would Mrs. Grady have them do? Nellie felt sick to her stomach. Reading out loud was the worst. Then she forgot even what she did know. The words stretched and shrank and danced. If only they would stay still for her!

"Charlene, you read this book—quietly, if you

please," Mrs. Grady continued. "Albert, you clean off the board—and do a good job this time, if you can. Harry, copy this paper over again. What a sloppy piece of work! Joe Lee, write out the words you missed on the test five times each. I'll come to the rest of you. Now, Ellen, what is your problem?"

Nellie moved over so that Mrs. Grady could squeeze into the seat with her. She smelled Mrs. Grady's flowery perfume and let out her breath with relief.

Mrs. Grady was trying. Even Nellie could see that. Her face was arranged in a smile but her foot was tapping, tapping, on the floor. She did not have much patience. Oh, she knew it! She would smile frostily in front of the class and say, "I'm afraid I just don't have much patience." She said it like it was something very good about her. She did not think it was a fault at all.

"Now, child, let's see what you know. Go slowly and try not to make any mistakes. This is a very easy book."

Nellie swallowed and began. "See the . . . boy . . . The boy has a . . ." The word looked like something she knew. She studied it closely.

Mrs. Grady cut in. "Toy. The boy has a toy."

"The boy has a toy. The boy is . . . big."

"Well, well," said Mrs. Grady. "I didn't think you'd get that." She tried to sound proud of Nellie but she did not quite make it.

Nellie began to sweat. "The boy is big," she read, her voice shaking. "The . . . toy is . . . big." She looked over to the next page. She wasn't getting anywhere reading this stuff! "See the toy. See the big toy."

Mrs. Grady stopped her. "All right, that's enough. Now take a look at this one and let's see what you can do with it."

She opened the new book. Nellie's heart beat faster and faster until it pounded inside her dress. Her hands began to sweat and her eyes watered until she could only see the pages hazily. Just when she was beginning to read the old book! Her hands shook as she turned the pages to get some idea of the awfulness ahead.

One thing, it was a new book, with fresh, clean pages. That was the first thing she noticed. Then she saw that there were no white houses and trees but old brick and brownstone houses and shops and black people on the streets. She turned the pages as slowly as she could, partly so she would stop sweating and shaking, partly because she really wanted to look at these people and what they were doing. There was one picture that went across both pages of a row of shops that looked almost like her own block. Maybe she could read the shop signs!

"Not so much time, Ellen. I have five other children to test this morning. Start, please."

Nellie turned back to the first page. "This is a . . ."

There was a long silence.

"City," Mrs. Grady said.

"This is a city. The city is . . . The . . city is . . . big. It is a big . . ."

"City," said Mrs. Grady.

"It is a big city." There! She had it now. She started all over again.

But Mrs. Grady closed the book. "After lunch today, Ellen, you will report to Room 111. A Reading Clinic is being set up for the slow readers. It might help you. Don't forget now, *immediately* after lunch period! Room 111."

The way she put it, Nellie stiffened at once. "What's this?" she mumbled. "I don't . . ." Then she stopped. At the same time, she wanted to go.

Mrs. Grady smiled in her thin way. "Good luck," she said before she went to sit with Dwayne and hear him read. He was even worse than Nellie was.

Nellie sat and listened to her head buzz with thoughts. For one thing, she would be out of this room for one period today, at the very least. They wouldn't have her go down there for less than one period. And that was plenty! She figured the rest would go ahead and take care of itself, no matter what. So she tucked it away in her head.

Mama had packed her a specially good lunch today, besides. That came first. She drummed her feet against the floor and Mrs. Grady turned around and gave her a mean look. Wide-eyed, Nellie smiled back.

chapter 4

IF THERE WAS ONE THING Nellie had learned from Mama it was that good news was just luck and could go away even faster than it came. You expected the bad and mostly you got it. When something good happened, you breathed very quietly not to hurt it. So Nellie gave no sign whatever when she walked into Room 111 and saw the woman sitting there.

Room 111 was the nicest room she had ever been in. Where had it come from? Deep blue rug on the floor. Pale blue paint on the walls. No more chipped green paint like only last week when the junior primary class was here. A whole row of bookshelves and books, low tables and chairs, and a few comfortable chairs like those Nellie had seen in the windows of furniture stores. She did not want to look at the lady sitting in one of those chairs, not just yet, so she looked at the pictures on the walls.

She was even more surprised. One picture of a woman ironing clothes looked almost like Mama. And there was another one of a woman sewing. And a woman pouring water. And a man riding a horse. They were things she knew—only they looked different. Almost more real. There was a long picture of a row of houses and stores going uphill and downhill along a street. Two different pictures of people playing cards. And one of some children jumping rope in a yard with a high fence.

"Hey," she said softly, surprised to words, "how come he done know of our yard?"

The voice behind her spoke quietly. "Well, there are plenty more like this one!"

Nellie half turned. "*I* wouldn't paint *this*, though."

"No? What would you paint then?"

Nellie stopped, confused. "Some trees, maybe. And flowers—lots of flowers. Pretty things."

Then she realized that she was talking. She looked down at the carpet on the floor.

The woman smiled. She was young and nicely plump and she smelled of perfume. "I'm Anne Lacey. And I believe you are Ellen Cameron, right?"

"I'm Nellie, that's who I am!"

"Nellie it shall be." And there was a pleasant silence.

Then Nellie smelled something else besides perfume.

Coffee. It smelled like home. Not like chalk and dust and school.

Miss Lacey showed her around the room and told her how it had been fixed up just for her clinic, with a coffeepot, refrigerator, and all the new furniture. Nobody in the school could say what was to go in it, only Miss Lacey. "And if anyone tells me what to do, that's the last they'll see of me!" It was her own room. Nellie could see that all right.

Then Miss Lacey was holding out a mug of hot coffee with a lot of milk and sugar, the way Nellie liked it. She sat down on one of the comfortable chairs. There was a silence again. Miss Lacey passed over some cookies and they both drank coffee and ate cookies without saying one word. It was like a fresh wind on a hot day in that room.

Finally, Miss Lacey said, "You'll come here every day at the same time, Nellie, probably for the rest of the school year. We're going to work together on your reading to make very sure you get into fourth grade in June and can read the way you should—and will."

Nellie had never heard anyone talk this way, except on the TV. Miss Lacey sounded like some kind of actress with her careful pronunciation, and it was funny being in the same room with her. Nellie almost wanted to laugh and she actually gave a little giggle half-smothered behind her hand.

Miss Lacey looked sharply at her, then decided to let

it pass and leaned back in her chair. "Matter of fact," she added, "now that I've met you, I can promise you that you'll be reading fourth grade books by June. How's that?"

"Unh-unh." Nellie shook her head. "They all say I'm dumb."

"Ha! I have to admit, you put on a good act, maybe you fool some people, eh?"

Nellie just kept shaking her head. She knew, as if she was seeing it before her, the report cards, the notes to Mama, all of them screaming *dumb dumb dumb*. Written on paper, loud and clear.

"No?" Miss Lacey said. "Well, we'll see. I'm going to make a small bet between the two of us. Agreed? If you learn to read, I'll give you a book as a prize. If you don't learn to read—what? I can't think. You can decide on that when the time comes—because it isn't going to come!"

Nellie let out her breath. She had not even realized she was holding it until that very moment when she thought she would burst. What had she been afraid of? This teacher had a lot to learn! "It don't make no difference anyhows."

"Doesn't it? Look me right in the eye and tell me that!"

But Nellie wouldn't. She grinned again. The chair was very cosy.

Then Miss Lacey said, "Well, good-bye for now, Nellie. I'll see you tomorrow."

Tomorrow was far away. LaVerne went home with Nellie after school and they made brownies, messed up the kitchen, giggled when Grace got after them to clean it up, and finally Grace began giggling, too. They scraped the bowl of the last bit of brownie mix, and all three of them cleaned the kitchen up together. When Mama came home and saw LaVerne, she invited her to supper at once and found one of Grace's old dresses she was saving for Nellie to fit LaVerne's long skinny frame.

Then when LaVerne went home, Mama asked all about her and kept shaking her head at what she heard. "I guess we be lucky just being together, an' don't you forget it, missy," she said when Nellie went to bed.

Only when she was lying in bed did Nellie remember the reading clinic. Had it really happened? Maybe there would be no clinic tomorrow. Maybe Miss Lacey was only saying she could come again. You could never tell with grownups.

When lunch was over the next day Nellie lingered behind the rest of her class. Perhaps some teacher would notice and tell her to hurry along now or she would be late. Then she would know that she was not supposed to go to see Miss Lacey and yesterday had been a mistake.

Her classmates marched up to the room. Nellie waited in the empty hall for someone to come after her. How strange she suddenly felt! Usually, no one was allowed in the halls without a pass. Every few minutes Mrs. Dewitt, the principal's secretary, popped out of her office like a jack-in-the-box to make sure the halls were clear. But no one noticed her now. The class bell rang. A quick, sharp silence settled on the building.

Then Nellie walked slowly down the long hall to its very end and around the corner to the short side. There it was, Room 111, with its door closed, looking very much as it always had. Nellie could tell nothing from the closed door. The halls were too quiet, too empty. All she could hear was her own breath.

She turned the knob. The door gave and she was in the room. Same as yesterday! Same blue rug. Same blue walls. She lifted her eyes and there was Miss Lacey, leaning back in her chair with an amused smile on her face.

"Can't make up your mind, Nellie? Good afternoon!"

"Yes'm," Nellie mumbled. "Mrs. Grady, she didn't say nothing today . . ."

"It was for *every* day, didn't you understand? Now, come on over here, we've got work to do!" Miss Lacey was very brisk. "First, take off your shoes. What's the matter, you've got holes in your socks? Well, who hasn't? Come along over here and stand against the wall." She was kind enough but Nellie did not like being hustled and moved here and there. She dragged her feet.

"Now onto the scale. Let's see . . . hmm. About right. What's the matter? Look! First thing we have to do is test you, you know, make sure your health is good."

"Nothing the matter with me!" Nellie said indignantly. "My Mama, she take good care of me!"

"*Your* Mama, yes. But you would be surprised at the children who can't work because they might be sick or hungry—and we have to find out. It's not just you!"

"All I sees in this room is me," Nellie said, looking around. "Hey, what's this?"

"Earphones. Sit right down at this table here and I'll put them on your ears."

"Huh! Not me!"

"Nonsense." She slipped the big earphones over Nellie's head. They jammed tight on her ears and she heard funny sounds through them.

Nellie sat stiffly, her eyes on Miss Lacey, who was pressing buttons and turning knobs like on the TV set. A sudden whooshing noise came into her ears, then a crackling sound, then a man's voice talking. She listened as hard as she could, but his words made no sense at all. "Starving, Harvard, vivid," he said, then more whooshing noise, then "livid, haven, carving," then his voice faded away while he was still talking nonsense like "rover, cavern, cloven," until she couldn't hear anymore.

Miss Lacey lifted the earphones away from her. Nellie heard every little sound in the room come to her ears bright and sharp. A window shade was faintly hitting

the frame. Miss Lacey's shoes slid across the rug. A knob turned with a muffled click, and the machine was shut off.

"Last word you could hear, Nellie, please."

"Huh? Oh . . . clo-ven," Nellie pronounced carefully.

"Good. Some other time I'll explain it all to you, we just don't have time now. Here, have some cookies—you want milk or coffee?—and I'll get the chart ready for your eye test. Ever had one before?"

"Coffee," said Nellie, "please. When I be real small, I think."

"Were you in school when you had your eyes tested?"

"Yes, ma'am. First grade."

Miss Lacey fiddled with things on her desk top while Nellie ate her cookies and drank the coffee, again made with much milk and sugar.

Nellie brushed the crumbs off the table top. That ear thing had been fun. "What I going to do now?"

"Just cover your left eye with this envelope and read from the chart. Tell me what you see."

"Letters," Nellie said, and giggled. Miss Lacey smiled back. Oh, Nellie knew her letters at least! "A C D B F G A O P K L V S A T, O again, P R, A again . . ."

"Now the right eye."

"Same letters? OK." She read them out once more.

"Anything blurry?"

"Only the last line, just a little."

"All right." Miss Lacey was marking things down on a sheet of paper. "This is your record, right here. No problems that I can see. Later on we'll have you checked out by a doctor and a dentist . . . now, don't get all excited, Nellie. Later on, not now."

"Nothing the matter with me!"

"We seem to be agreed on that, at any rate." Miss Lacey smiled again. Nellie wanted to lose herself right into that wide, warm smile. Miss Lacey looked beautiful and strange to her, not like anyone she had ever met. Her hair was pulled back into a great puff at her neck. Long silver earrings hung from her ears and made a tiny pleasant *chink* when she turned her head. Her eyes did not look blank or tired but were filled with amusement sometimes and at other times were wary and cool. She caught Nellie's glance and put her hand up to pat her hair.

Then their time was up.

Going back to her class, Nellie felt the way she did when she came out of the bathroom at home after soaking for a long time in the tub. After the cozy feeling of that snug warm room, she had to take a deep breath and wait a minute to get used to the regular things going on.

Not that she had really *liked* the hour today, with all those tests and Miss Lacey pushing her around—not *really* liked. Still, coming out of the room, she felt clean and fresh, as if she had just had a bath, and she missed the warmth of the blue rug and the fresh walls when she was transported back to the chipped paint and the dusty maps.

After school she told Sam about the special program, "not just for me, see, only I was picked for it an' I going to be learning things."

"About time they got something going in this school," was all he said. Then he started talking about his problems in finding one teacher in that place who could help him with the algebra he was studying on his own. "They can't even *read* the stuff right, and not one of them knows how to do it. They're ashamed to admit it, you know."

Sam discouraged her. Algebra! Where would *she* be next to that? Slowly the nice warm feeling oozed away from her. At home she did her homework so quietly that Ramona wondered if she were sick.

"Being so good not like you, Nell."

"Leave me alone!" Nellie screamed.

"Who you talking to like that?" Ramona asked, then socked her.

Grace looked up from her romance magazine. "I'm gonna tell Mama what you be doing, I'm gonna tell Mama, see if I ain't." Ramona socked Grace, too, and Grace pulled at Ramona's hair until the braid came undone.

Jesse was crying at the fight when Mama walked in, Grace was yelling, and Ramona was screaming, "That why I gots to get outta this house! I ain't got no respect here, the way they treat me an' all. Tell 'em, Mama, ain't I in charge?" Then Ramona added some words Mama said she'd rather die than hear from anyone, least of all her very own child.

Nellie thought about Miss Lacey and her quiet ways. But she didn't say one single word in the middle of the fight. Not one. Maybe tomorrow. She did not want to throw it all out into the noise and anger. She wanted to hug it to herself as a secret, something that belonged to her alone.

chapter 5

OF COURSE, that didn't mean she rushed right on down to Room 111 the next day. By lunchtime she had begun to wonder again and to doubt and her stomach was achy and she went to the bathroom and stayed there a long time, washing her hands and patting down her hair. Compared to Miss Lacey she looked downright *bad!*

She opened the door of the girls' bathroom and peered out into the empty hall. She was seeing the school differently, almost the way it looked when nobody was around to disturb the stillness.

"Hey, you, girl! Get back into your class, hear? Which class are you?"

Nellie jumped back. Mrs. Dewitt was bearing down on her. She grasped the shoulder of Nellie's dress good and tight and just stood there. "Well, what's your business in this hall?"

"Clinic," Nellie mumbled.

"Clinic? No health clinics here today far as I know—and I *know!* Speak up!"

"Reading clinic," Nellie whispered.

Mrs. Dewitt released her. "Oh, *that* thing! Hurry along then, we can't have loitering in these halls!"

Mrs. Dewitt didn't move until Nellie went on down the hall, turned, and disappeared into the other corridor.

The door to Room 111 was open and Nellie walked right in. "That Miz Dewitt! You know her? She an old witch!"

"Oh, good afternoon, Nellie. You mean that old gal in the office? Yes, I know her. I try to stay out of her way."

"Me, too!" Nellie agreed, plunking herself down on the closest chair. She looked around the room to see if anything had changed.

Miss Lacey smiled. "No tests today, Nellie. In fact, I thought we might just talk a little. You know, you hardly said one word on Monday, that's why I thought perhaps you couldn't hear too well."

"Oh, I can talk plenty! Ramona, she my sister, she say I talk too much, Mrs. Grady she tell me I rattle on like a sewing machine. I never had no problem talking!"

"So I can see! Good, I like children who speak up."

"You the onliest one then!"

"Let's be friends and just talk to each other. How about it?"

Nellie shook Miss Lacey's hand but she wasn't so sure. What Mama had said was something to keep in mind. Could she trust Miss Lacey with even a piece of her self? Sam had made a mistake with Mrs. Webster and he was good and smart. So she kept a smile on her face but said nothing.

"Have you always lived in Washington, Nellie?"

"Yes'm."

"In the same place?"

"Oh, no! Nobody lives in the same place long around here, don't you know that?"

"No, I didn't. Why not?"

"Zillion things! They tear the houses down. People comes and goes. . . ." Nellie ended vaguely.

"Some people don't pay rent?" Miss Lacey asked.

"Naw! No one I knows. You know folks like that?"

"Some. Right here in this school, maybe."

"No one I knows, no one at all!" Good thing she hadn't said anything—Mama was right!

"All right," Miss Lacey said. "Come on and have a snack and look at these new books. Just came today!" They didn't talk then, only ate and looked at the pages of color photographs, one more attractive than the next. Each book was different. One had pictures of children playing, black children, jumping rope, playing stickball, riding bikes, throwing a basketball, running, playing hopscotch and stoop ball and a lot of other games.

Nellie grinned when she saw those pictures but she knew that Miss Lacey's eyes were on her, so she said nothing. When they looked at the book of country pictures, she pointed out the trees and flowers and showed Miss Lacey that she knew the words for meadow and cloud even if she couldn't read them.

"Would you like to live in the country like that, Nellie?"

"Yes'm, if my Mama and Daddy was with me," she said, without giving anything more away.

"You like Washington, too?"

"It OK. You like it?"

"Oh, it's a beautiful city! I think I'm going to enjoy going to all the famous places. Have you been to any of them?"

Nellie shook her head.

"Not to the White House? What about the Washington Monument?"

"Oh, that big tall thing? I been there—but we didn't go up top."

"Do you ever go downtown? To shop or see a movie?"

"Not me. My Mama, she go sometimes, Ramona and Grace, they be my big sisters, they go all the time, but I stays on my block mostly, I gots my friends there—I gots a lot of friends, you know!"

"Good for you!" Miss Lacey said just a little too

warmly. Nellie looked up at her again. The teacher's enthusiasm was tiring her out. So much talk about nothing!

But Miss Lacey wasn't going to stop. "Washington is supposed to be the most beautiful city in the country, you know."

"I likes it. My Daddy, he like to go fishing, he say fishing ain't so good here anymore on the river. Once he brought home a basket of herring real early on a Saturday, just took off working to go, and my Mama, she fried 'em all up for breakfast and they was the bestest fish we ever had. Only once he did it." Remembering that, Nellie forgot Miss Lacey for the moment and smiled a wide, impish smile.

"I wish you would tell me a story about that, will you? Next week, all right? Once we get started on our real work. How would that be?"

Miss Lacey kept pushing her, without waiting one single second for a space where a person might breathe. It was very hard to make up your mind, Nellie thought, with so much good and bad all mixed in together. She'd have to think on it at night in her bed before she went to sleep, when she could be alone. "Oh, yes, ma'am, fine," she said enthusiastically to Miss Lacey. "Next week."

And because she was so confused she thought she'd wait before saying anything to Mama. If she let on how mixed up she was, maybe Mama would make the school take her out of the clinic. And she didn't want that, leastways not so soon.

chapter 6

BY FRIDAY AFTERNOON Nellie had put Miss Lacey right out of her mind. No school thing, good or bad, stayed in her head after three o'clock on Friday! Besides, Sunday school was starting again, and Nellie wanted to save room to think about that. This would be her first year in real Sunday school, not baby classes with colored pictures and Bible stories.

Sister Spry, who took the younger children last year, was a sad old lady who shouted "Hallelujah!" a lot but didn't say much else that Nellie could remember. But this year, Sister Painter would be in charge, and for her alone Nellie would have been eager. For one thing her first name was Nina, and Nellie thought Nina was the most beautiful name she had ever heard, not at all like the names of everyone else Nellie knew. Second, Mrs. Painter was from the West Indies and Nellie could listen to her soft, almost singing speech all day every day. Oooh, that Sister Painter was something! Nellie knew her class would just have to be different.

She thought about what it would be like before she went to sleep that night, lying in her folding bed close to the floor and wondering, half-awake and drowsy, but she soon had to stop because she really didn't *know!*

Then Saturday was upon her, full of cleaning and shopping and rushing around. She kept the question of Sister Painter in her mind like an itch that had to be scratched; maybe there would be time after supper to talk to Mama about it.

Saturday night was a wild time—baths, hair washing, ironing, money counted up, and everyone hopping around at once, it seemed to Nellie. Mama said, "Yes, yes," and patted her on the arm absently while she checked on the soup and the custard. "Sam, you give Jesse a bath, then you can hop into the same tub and clean yourself. That be two of you fresh for Sunday. Then, let me see . . . Ramona and Grace, later on you can be washing your hair in the shower, the hot water come back in then. How that be? Best way, it seem to me. Meanwhiles, you be doing the ironing for tomorrow."

Ramona burst out, "Mama, I wanted to go on out,

can't I be the first? You doing it this way special to keep me home!"

Daddy looked up from the newspaper. "Awful things going on, here, read 'em yourself. Saturday night ain't no time for you on the streets, no time a-tall. Your Mama be right, girl."

But Ramona would not subside. She grumbled and complained and slammed around her room and picked a fight with Grace. "You ever going to pick your head up from your romance magazine, little sister?" she said in her rough voice.

"Aw, shut up! You jealous, you ain't got no boy-friends like you with your big fresh mouth!"

Nellie went into the front room and turned the TV on good and loud so as not to hear the screaming. When she came back into the kitchen to try and talk to Mama, Grace and Mama were giggling together over the new pink dress Grace had bought with her baby-sitting money.

"You surely in love," Mama teased. "Pink dress! Remind me when I was a girl. You coming along right nice, Grace, the way you do your hair an' all."

Willie was brushing himself up to go out. "I'll be through in a minute!" he called from the bathroom. When he was finished, Sam and Jesse went in. "Mama, how I look?"

"Always fine to me, son. New shoes?"

Willie looked down at the shiny black wingtips with their raised heel and narrow pointed toe. "Yah. Friend of mine at work, he know a good place, like 'em?"

Daddy looked up again. "You gots more shoes to your feet, Willie, than sense to your head, ask me."

Willie ducked his head and quickly pulled his wallet out. "Here, Mama, my board." It was ten dollars.

"Thank you, son. Don't get in no trouble now, we looking for you to come home in one piece, see? Watch out!"

Mama said the same thing every Saturday. Willie never even answered.

Sitting at the kitchen table, Nellie was thinking about tomorrow, about Sunday school, about Sister Painter, about her own excitement, and the more she thought about it all, the dreamier she got and the more she felt she *had* to talk to someone. All around her was swirling activity and chatter. She sat small in her chair, wondering and humming to herself, a comforting, tuneless hum. What would it be like tomorrow? Like Mrs. Grady, all bad? Like Miss Lacey, confusing and troubling?

Mama's voice broke into her thoughts. "Nell, we get you all clean an' washed tomorrow morning, we gots time. Scoot off to bed now, you just in the way here almost falling asleep."

"Mama? Mama, can I call Emma? I *gots* to talk to her."

Mama looked closely at her. "Emma? Still missing

her? Want me to dial for you?"

"No, I can do it," Nellie said, a little uncertainly. Mama had always helped her dial before.

"No reason why you can't, lamb. Just be careful now."

Nellie pulled the phone off the table by Mama and Daddy's bed and sat down in the corner under the table with the phone in her lap. No one could see her or hear her. It was dark and quiet and warm. She had Emma's phone number on a scrap of paper stuck in Mama's mirror frame and she dialed slowly and carefully, her heart beating fast with each ring of the phone. When Emma answered, she sighed deeply and stretched out her legs on the floor.

"It's me. Nellie. Guess what? I called you by myself."

Emma laughed. "Honest, Nell, you are a funny one!"

Nellie explained. "I mean, I dialed an' all." She was a little hurt. "By myself. I was wondering if I was right, you see."

Emma's voice on the phone sounded different, muffled and far away. It was like talking to another person entirely. "Well, here I am, so you did right. How's things?"

Now that Emma was really asking her, Nellie did not know quite what to say. Dreaming had been easier. "Sunday school be starting tomorrow, Emma. You excited?"

"Nell, listen, I'm not coming. My Gran, she got converted to another church, she singing and praying, you never heard anything like it! She don't want me to go back to Zion, she say it ain't got the fullness of truth."

"Oh, Emma!" Even the Sunday school would be a little spoiled now. "I was going to tell you tomorrow, we gots this special program at our school an' I be picked to go in it!"

Emma's voice was warm and happy. "Oh, I be glad for you, Nell! I'm a grade higher now, they skipped me ahead an' the work be hard but it keep me busy, and my Gran be right pleased, she say that because she been converted to the truth faith." Emma chuckled with her deep, rich laughter.

They talked for a while longer but Emma grew fainter and further away until by the end of the conversation she was hardly there at all. Everything would be changed this year, it seemed, and Emma belonged to last year after all, even though Nellie did not want to let her go.

chapter 7

SUNDAY SCHOOL MET in the afternoon for one hour. Then there was an hour of quiet games or time to look at books in the church library. Sometimes a missionary visitor would show films. Then the women would lay out food for everyone, and that was the best part of all—sandwiches and cookies, fruit and pie, and brimming pitchers of cold milk.

Sister Painter was small and slight and she hopped and skipped and bounced rather than walked. "I come from the country of Anansi the spiderman," she said, explaining her bouncy energy. She bounced right up to the front of the room as if she weren't new at all, and gave everyone her quick smile.

Nellie remembered when Mrs. Painter had been converted and had joined the church only a year or so ago. She had started to work for the church at once, doing everything she could, rushing around day and night to help. Preacher Evans had been mighty glad. Mama called her "a sainted soul" and went out one night a week to work with one of Mrs. Painter's groups mending baby clothes to give out in layettes.

Mrs. Painter was married to a dentist who had his office near the church, a quiet man with a thin mustache who was as slow-moving as his wife was quick. He had always done work for people who couldn't pay much but now he kept open on Fridays from noon until late in the evening just doing clinic work for church members, and he wouldn't let anyone pay him at all but told them to put the money into the social action fund.

All the Camerons had gone for dental work and were still going, some one time and some another. Nellie did not much care for the smell of Dr. Painter's office or the feel of the dental chair, or anything to do with the pain of having her teeth filled, but Mama called it the Lord's providence that Dr. Painter was staying in the neighborhood and working for them, and Mama did not take lightly to the sin of refusing the Lord's providence. So Nellie went.

But that was Dr. Painter. Here was Mrs. Painter, smiling down at them, maybe forty in all, sitting on metal folding chairs and making a racket. Oh, they were all there, boys on one side and girls on the other, banging their feet and talking, wondering just what Mrs. Painter would say.

Out of habit Nellie turned to look for Emma. She checked every face in the classroom and then she remembered. Emma wouldn't be coming anymore.

Mrs. Painter tapped with a ruler on the chalkboard and frowned because she did not have silence. "Children!" she said. "I am nothing but a poor instrument of the Lord, a servant of Jesus. I doesn't claim to be more than that, what He let me be. But since I am here for that, you are here to listen to me and maybe, just maybe, the Lord will come and speak to you, directly into your heart like He spoke to me and made my life a song."

She paused. Some scuffling, but not much. So she went on. "I'm doing this school somewhat different now. I'm going to begin straight in talking about the Bible, talking about God, talking about you!" Nellie felt Mrs. Painter was looking straight at her. Blinking, she looked back, solemn as could be.

"Some people say you are children, and stories is good enough for you. Now stories is fine, I aim to tell you some myself every week, but stories is not enough, not for children like you are, knowing the way life is in your bones. You need more than that. When a baby is little, he drinks his mother's milk, but then he grows and milk, which is good in itself, still is not enough to feed him.

"So we are going to look at the Psalms this year,

which are the prayers to God, like our hymns, and we are going to wrestle with those Psalms like Jacob and the angel, until we make some sense out of them that you can carry out this door and onto those cold streets outside.

"Now, listen! In Psalm 80 it says the words: 'But him I would feed on the marrow of the wheat, and I would fill him with honey out of the rock.' What does this mean? Can anyone tell me?" No answer. "All right! Listen some more. Last year you heard the story of Samson. What happened when he met the lion? Come on now, speak out. You, Josie Strickland!"

Josie was a string bean of a girl with little pigtails sticking out all around her head. She whispered her answer. "Samson killed that lion."

"And that he did!" said Mrs. Painter with satisfaction. "Samson killed that lion. Then what?"

"I know, I know!" Terry Hunt's hand was waving. "Honey, it came from that lion."

Mrs. Painter nodded her head. "Honey from the body of the lion." She was talking so quietly now that Nellie thought she was talking more to herself than to them. "Well, children, I was reading Psalm 80 just the other morning, not intending to begin with it today but with another one, an easier one the books say, as if any prayer to God can be easy, but I thought of Samson and the honey from the lion and the more I thought and wondered, the more I decided to come today with those words and let us all wonder together. Now, what does that mean: honey out of the rock?"

She looked at them. They all looked back at her.

"What does it mean, the marrow of the wheat? Come, children, help me here. Talk about wheat."

"It grows," said one boy.

"It is in the fields," said a girl who sat next to Nellie.

"It is beautiful," Nellie said.

Mrs. Painter nodded again. "Yes, yes, Lord, yes, you are right. Here is the farmer with his seed wheat." She drew some small kernels on the chalkboard. "He plants it, then he weeds the field, and prays for rain, and the wheat grows."

"Man, that chopping weeds is hard," one boy exclaimed.

"Oooh, hard work is right!" Mrs. Painter said. "But then the wheat comes up out of the ground, it grows its golden self into the sun, it gets higher and higher." She drew an ear of wheat on the chalkboard. "Then what happens?"

"Gets picked."

"Harvested, you mean," one small voice corrected the other.

"Harvested," said Mrs. Painter. "Anyone seen such a harvest?"

No one had.

"Big machines harvest it now, but once it was done by hand, by man working hard again. Like in the story of

Ruth. All right, harvested. Then what?"

No one knew.

Mrs. Painter shook her head. "Threshed is the word. Got to get that wheat kernel free from all that is around it, like the soul got to be freed from sin. Before the big machines came, that meant more hard work, men standing and beating up and down upon that wheat."

She lifted her arms high above her head, her hands holding an imaginary flail, and brought them down.

"Hard work! All hard work. Then here is that wheat, winnowed and threshed, sitting in bags, waiting. Waiting to go to the mill. Old mills had big grindstones, ground that wheat down fine between them, like the Lord grind your souls, make them fine enough for His table. More hard work! Then that flour get mixed with other things into dough, dough get baked in a hot fire, and finally out come bread, the marrow of the wheat.

"Oooh, children, I'll tell you what that mean! Jesus promise to feed you and He keep that promise until the end of the world. But one thing He did not promise is to make that feeding easy. Good bread is the staff of life, but from wheat to bread is work, beating, grinding, burning. *That* is what Jesus meant, children! And you, too, each one of you, yes, every last one, you are the wheat and Jesus make you into the bread for His table, but first He got to put you through the fire of life, through the beating and the grinding and the burning. And you already know something of that, young as you are. Never forget, children, from this suffering come the good bread which is your soul living life eternal in paradise!"

Nobody stirred. They had never heard such talk before directed right to them, not like Preacher Evans, who seemed to talk just to have the words roll out on his tongue. Mrs. Painter was sweating. She wiped her face and sat down, fanning herself.

Nellie felt a stirring behind the indifference she put on before the world. She was taken out of her preoccupation with herself and her misery, listening to Mrs. Painter, and she was thrilled at the thought that all her troubles with schoolwork would get her into heaven. Somehow. If she only paid attention to Mrs. Painter, maybe she would learn how.

Mrs. Painter was talking again, in a low caressing voice now. "Honey out of the rock, honey out of the lion. Let us think about that, children. What is a rock?"

"Hard."

"Yes. And what is a lion?"

"Scary!"

"So it is. Yet the Lord say honey come out of a rock, honey come out of a lion, and the Lord never wrong. How can that be? Honey now, honey is sweet, sweet as the word of the Lord whispering in the heart. How do the word of the Lord come into the heart? Children, I'll tell you! It come out of the rock, out of the lion, for that is the world, the everyday world we finding on the

street, the world that is the rock, for it is hard, and the lion, for it is scary. But the word of the Lord is sweet like honey. Yes, that is how it is."

Mrs. Painter came down close to them. She sat on a folding chair so she could look right at them, each and every one.

"Now," Mrs. Painter was saying, "tell me about honey. Someone!" There was a silence. "Where does it come from?"

Nellie knew that! "Bees," she said, looking down at the floor.

"Bees?" said a boy she did not know. "You crazy! It come from jars in the Safeway, I be seeing it myself."

Mrs. Painter came up right close to Nellie. "Bees is so right, child. You know any more about bees?"

Nellie shook her head *no*, then she said, "Yes," just the second after. Where had she heard? From a letter that Uncle Gar had written to Mama? From something Brother Williams and Daddy talked about? Was she even right?

Mrs. Painter was looking right down into her eyes and Mrs. Painter's soft brown hand was cupping Nellie's chin. "You going to tell us about bees, child, come right on and do it. Some people," she said, with a look at the boy who had called Nellie crazy, "don't even know what they *don't* know."

Nellie took a deep breath. "Bees, they lives in their own houses, hives they is called. I remember now! My uncle, he have some bees, so he make his own honey. The bees makes it, I mean." She stopped and took another deep breath. Then she giggled. "My uncle write that the sweeter the honey, the more them bees rushing around guarding it, the harder they sting if you not careful. The sting, that go with the sweet honey, you gets 'em both together."

Mrs. Painter laughed back, freely and happily. "Child, what *is* your name?"

"Nellie, I Sister Cameron's child."

"Well, Nellie, you said it exactly right, what I was going to say myself, and there you went and said it. The honey and the sting go together, you cannot have one without the other. Do you know what that means?"

But Nellie didn't hear any more of the lesson, nor what anyone said. Mrs. Painter's sweet voice came through almost like a song and touched Nellie's bliss but did not break it. She sat for the rest of the hour with a fixed smile on her face and her palms sweaty and the words swept by her ears without resting for one single moment. She did not even realize that the time was up until she heard the folding chairs clatter around her.

On the chalkboard Mrs. Painter had written: "Psalm 80, verse 17: But him I would feed on the marrow of the wheat, and I would fill him with honey out of the rock."

"One more thing, children," Mrs. Painter was saying, her voice low and tense, "each person has his own rock blocking his way. Each person try to strike his rock so honey come out. For next week, you learn that verse by heart, then you write down for me on a piece of paper *your* rock so this year we work and pray together and make honey come out of it for *you*."

Then Mrs. Painter smiled across the other children straight to Nellie. "I think you should begin right today collecting picture cards, Nellie, don't you? Giving me such a smart answer! You are a credit to your mother," and she put into Nellie's hand a small card with a colored picture of a bright gold moon against a black night, and the words, "You have made the moon to mark the seasons."

"Do you like it, Nellie? I chose new cards this year."

Nellie nodded, hardly able to breathe.

And when Ramona came to pick her up after the games hour and the snack, Nellie showed her the beautiful picture. "I was the smartest today, Sister Painter say so!"

Ramona looked amused. "God sure performing wonders today, hallelujah!" she said.

"You be jealous, Ramona, 'cause you don't get nothing!"

"Honey, that a nice picture an' I be glad for you, an' Mama, she be right proud. I just teasing, you look so serious an' all. Like this!" And Ramona made her round face into a puffed-out moon with rolling eyes. Nellie laughed, then Ramona laughed, then they both giggled together all the way home.

chapter 8

THE FIRST THING Nellie saw on Monday morning was Grace talking to herself in the mirror. "Good morning, how are you?" Grace said very carefully to her face in the mirror.

"You're cracking up, for sure!" Ramona called down from the top bunk. "Watch out, Nellie, I'm coming down! Get into Grace's bunk, why don't you, so we can get your bed outta the way."

"Wish I could sleep in your bunk," Nellie mumbled sleepily.

"When they come to carry Grace off to the nut house, you get *her* bunk, how's that? What you be doing, Gracie?"

"Fine, thank you," Grace was saying to herself in the

mirror. Then she smiled. "I have made two decisions . . ."

"On Monday *morning?*" Ramona interrupted.

"Two decisions," Grace repeated. Now she was getting dressed while she talked. "I have decided that I like
Otis Redding better than Ray Charles . . ."

"Well, hallelujah!" Ramona interrupted again. "Such
fancy talk! You forget your brains? Hey, Nellie, look
on the pillow, Grace's brains lying there somewheres?"

"Funny, funny," Grace said loftily, brushing her hair.
"I have also decided to be a teacher, and *you* mayn't
know it, Ramona, but you cannot be a teacher without
you speak just right."

Ramona snorted. "How those teachers get in *my*
school, then, tell me that, if you so smart? Some of 'em
don't speak no kind of right."

"Huh! I can see I won't get any sympathy in *this*
family!" Grace said. "I'm going into the bathroom to
get washed now, if you all don't mind." And she
flounced out of the bedroom.

When they were getting ready to leave for school,
Nellie slipped over to Grace and tugged at her hand.
"You can tell me, Gracie, I be glad you going to teach.
Maybe you be helping me." Nellie saw Jesse start out
the door. "Hey, Jesse, wait for me, don't be going
alone!"

"You are a funny little thing!" Grace said, just as
Emma had.

Nellie did not think she was funny. Jesse, maybe; after all, he was a baby. But she was a big girl, at least she *thought* so. It always seemed to go like that. As soon as she had something about herself all set in her mind, somebody broke it apart. Now *that* was funny, but *she* wasn't funny at all.

"Only one thing, Grace," Nellie called back over her shoulder as she pelted down the street after Jesse, "I don't like Otis Redding a-tall!" She did not hear if Grace answered her.

"Come along, Jesse," Sam said, hurrying the little boy, who wanted to walk on steps and copings. "Just when Nellie gets better in the morning, you get worse."

"Me?" asked Nellie.

"Oh, there you are! You, what?"

"Getting better, I mean."

"Almost cheerful, *I* mean. And here is Jesse crying and going slow—we're gonna be late. Come *on!*"

Jesse ran to keep up. He did not make a sound, but tears ran down his cheeks. Nellie held tight to his hand to comfort him as she walked him to the door of Yolanda Harris, the woman who baby-sat for him. Nellie did not like Mrs. Harris herself but she had to make believe for Jesse's sake.

"Oh, you here!" Mrs. Harris said when she opened the door. She was a heavy light-skinned lady with a frown always on her face. "Must you ring the bell so hard, child? Your mama is such a nice lady, how come you children make so much noise?"

"I be quiet," Jesse whispered, gulping.

"You don't say," Mrs. Harris said, motioning him in. "News to me, that is. Best not to let your mama know, though, is what I say. Well, girl, don't stand there! Run on off or you'll be late. Your brother's gone already."

And Nellie was late. Only a minute but Mrs. Grady made the most of it, and reminded her that she was in a special program and could be taken out of it just like *that!*

Nellie said nothing. She looked at the floor and kept herself to herself. Anyway, Mrs. Grady didn't say a word about actually *taking* her away from the reading clinic. Good! She relaxed her toes inside her shoes. School was like a nut. You threw away the shell and kept the good inside. And you hoped that the inside would be sweet, not bitter the way nuts sometimes were.

"I'm in a special program," she bragged to LaVerne at lunchtime, eating her peanut butter sandwich. "You got to get *put* in it."

"Yeah? Not me. They done give up on me, Nellie, like my Ma."

"Well, truth to tell, it ain't so much, LaVerne. Just reading an' things. I didn't even tell my Mama about it."

"Think she'd listen? My Ma, she wouldn't, not her! I tell you what, this Christmas I'm gonna ask her to send me to my Grandma down in Alabama, and if she don't do it, why, I'm gonna run away to her and just stay there and never come back here."

Nellie almost started to say something about Mrs. Painter, then she closed her mouth and stood staring.

"You look like a fish with your eyes popping and your mouth open an' close, a dumb fish!"

In some ways Nellie was scared of LaVerne. She wished once again that Emma Rice was still at school with her. Emma would understand everything. OK. Maybe not everything. Only she looked so smart, with her face all closed up and her quiet ways.

But LaVerne, the way she looked at you with her hard eyes, suddenly you felt silly and wanted to shut up. So now Nellie wasn't too sure about the reading clinic, even though she had been sure after Sunday school yesterday.

When she had finished every last bit of her lunch, she walked very slowly to Room 111. Mama had sliced a banana to put with the usual peanut butter between bread, and Nellie still had the strange, good taste in her mouth.

Miss Lacey was grinning when she walked in. She waited until Nellie closed the door behind her, then she went over to a machine and touched a button. Nellie stopped stock still, caught up in her own thoughts. Out of the wall she heard a soft voice saying, "Hey, how come he done know of our yard?" and it was her voice, saying those very words she had spoken the first time she was in this room!

"Like that?" Miss Lacey asked, still grinning.

"Hey, how'd you do it?" Nellie was not even sure she liked it. Her very own voice somewhere without her!

Miss Lacey had coffee and cookies ready. She laughed pleasantly as she settled down in her chair.

"I promise I'll show you how to use the tape recorder," she said, "if you read this for me."

Nellie looked at the paper with the same old sinking feeling that made her sick. She tasted banana and peanut butter again, and this time it was not a good taste. She hated all the squiggly marks that ran all over the paper like bugs. This was her rock, sure enough. Suppose she just couldn't learn?

Nellie took a deep breath and looked again. "Hey," she read, "how . . ." Then she looked up at Miss Lacey the way she looked at all her teachers, to see in her face if the words were right or not. But Miss Lacey was giving all her attention to the cookies. "Go on," she said, brushing the crumbs from her dress.

Why wasn't Miss Lacey helping her? Suddenly Nellie felt angry at this woman who was supposed to care but who didn't, not really, for all her words, not like Mrs. Painter, who sweated and looked right into your eyes. It wasn't fair, Miss Lacey not helping her. "I'm not going to," she said stubbornly. "I'm going back to my room. You can't keep me here!"

Miss Lacey looked up sharply. "Well, I certainly can, if you want to know! But I wouldn't if you really wanted to go back to your room, you can bet on that!

The door's not locked, Nellie. Go and open it if you want. There's plenty of children who'd want your hour —and use it. Am I wrong? Don't you really want to read?"

"Yes, ma'am," Nellie whispered.

Miss Lacey seemed not to have heard. "Well, listen here, then, missy, don't try to fool me with those sweet little ways and that shy little voice and how nice you are and all the rest. You don't fool me, not one bit. You're angry, girl, and you're scared and you're just as shook-up as you can be. And I don't care, not about one thing or the other. All I care about is: are you going to work for me? 'Cause if not, I'll go get another girl for this hour."

"Well, if I gotta stay . . ."

"No got to about it, Nellie. This is up to you. It's your work and you'll know when you can read that it's because of you. Because *you* can do it."

"But I can't. I thought you would help me."

"Well, maybe," Miss Lacey said. "Maybe. But not much, and only if you need it."

Nellie grew panicky. "But I do! I need lots of help, and I don't have much time. They gonna leave me back, and my Mama'll cry and my Daddy'll whip me sure. And Sam'll never let up teasing me."

"So that's the way it is, is it? Who is this Sam?"

"My brother Sam. He be ashamed of me," she whispered. "He not the only one. They're right, too."

She did not look at Miss Lacey at all. But she told her, just the same, about Jesse, who never left off bothering her, about high-and-mighty Grace and Ramona, and about Willie with his teasing. About Mama and Daddy.

Miss Lacey never said a word. Maybe that was why Nellie found she could talk about her family as she had never done before. She could almost forget Miss Lacey and simply talk out into the room until she had said everything on her mind.

When she was finished, Miss Lacey said, "Why, honey, is that all? You surely can learn to read before the end of this year. Whyever not?"

She looked so certain that Nellie could think of no answer right then. "I got to get help," she repeated.

"Maybe you won't need any. But I'm not exactly running away now, am I? You're just getting worked up for nothing, I guess. Right?"

"I guess you right," Nellie mumbled. It was an answer she had made maybe a million times to a thousand people. She never believed it herself. But the words filled up the silence.

"Well, then, have something to drink and let's start then. We are wasting mighty good time."

Nellie sighed and looked at the paper again. She felt very tired. "Hey," she read, "how come he . . ." Nellie stopped. She knew these words! She read on, slurring in her haste: "Hey, how come he done know of our yard?"

Miss Lacey was amused. "Good for you! Now come

over here and let's see how this tape recorder works."

She showed Nellie how the spools of tape moved and how to flip the switch on and off. She showed her the microphone that could pick a voice up from anywhere in the room. Nellie flipped the switch several times. Then she went back to the start of the spool and turned it on again.

"Hey, how come he done know of our yard?" she heard. Then, "Well, there are plenty more like this one!"

She turned the machine off again and looked down at the paper in her hand. "Well," she read, "there are plenty more like this one!"

Nellie felt like screaming and running around. She didn't. She went right on listening and reading until she got to the end. No trouble now!

Then she played the tape over again. Nobody had ever cared enough for her words to do anything with them but let them vanish into the air. Now she felt funny inside as she thought of those words kept forever in Miss Lacey's room. Not that they were such good words. She would do better. But this was something!

"Can I keep this?" she asked shyly, showing Miss Lacey the typed paper.

Miss Lacey brought out a folder with gold letters pasted on it: *By Nellie Cameron.*

"Like it?" she asked, smiling.

At first Nellie said nothing. She felt the shiny gold paper of the letters. She opened it and saw the fasteners hidden inside the stiff paper cover. "What's it for? Is it mine?"

"Exactly!" Miss Lacey said. "I made it just for you. I hope you like the way I designed it—if not, you can change it."

Nellie shook her head. She liked the folder just as it was, with her name in those big gold letters. "It's beautiful," she whispered.

"Now this paper you read from," Miss Lacey continued, "it's yours, it goes right in here. You'll tell stories and I'll type them up and they'll go in, too. It'll be your book. How about it?"

They slipped the paper inside.

Then Miss Lacey herself took out a book and read to Nellie about a poor girl in a small town in the South with big dreams of her own. The hour was over too soon. "You'll have to tell me a story tomorrow, now remember!"

That night Nellie hid away in Mama's room and called Emma again.

"Hi, Nell! I been thinking of you today, honest. What's new? My Gran bought me colored paper an' I be making doll clothes like we usta."

Nellie sighed with pleasure. "Ooh, Emma, I wish we could be doing it together. Not much fun when I be alone."

Last year they had spent many hours making two

paper dolls from brown paper bags glued onto shirt cardboard. Grace had teased them but in the end she had helped draw them and had made sure they were just perfect, with the right expressions on their faces and shapely little feet at the end of their legs. Emma and Nellie had named them, after a lot of discussion, and they were delighted with the grown-up sound of the names they had chosen. Francina and Melendie.

They played with the dolls all year, making up games and stories, having Francina and Melendie go to wonderful places like theaters or airports, places they wanted to see. But when Emma moved and took Melendie with her, the fun was gone. So Nellie had finally put Francina away carefully in her dresser drawer.

Now Nellie sat on the edge of the bed, listening to Emma on one side and to the faint noises in the rest of the apartment on the other side. Emma was making Melendie a blue coat with a fur collar and matching boots with fur trim.

"Wish I'd thought of that," Nellie said. Then she remembered something she could tell Emma about. "Listen! I be writing a book!"

"About Francina and Melendie?"

"Not them! I mean, I wasn't going to, but maybe I will now you said that. I was just going to be writing things for this teacher in my special class. But Emma, that be a good idea!"

In the middle of all this talk, she could not fit all her

news about Mrs. Painter and the colored picture from
Sunday school and the whole story about Miss Lacey
and the reading clinic, but she didn't care. Francina and
Melendie! What could be better? She would write a million stories and never once talk about herself!

"Nellie, you going to get off that phone? I be expecting a call!" Grace shouted through the door.

Nellie made a face at her sister and said good-bye to
Emma. She could see Emma's face at the other end of
the telephone line just as clear as if she were in the room
with her. "Some teacher!" she said to Grace. "You calling your boyfriend, that's what."

"You keep on so fresh, you *never* have a boyfriend!"

"Don't be so sure," Nellie called back. "I got lots of
things you not be knowing about!"

chapter 9

NELLIE FOUND a thousand reasons for not telling Mama and Daddy about the clinic. Mainly, she wanted something big to astonish them, and through November each day was only a little day, not special, sometimes good and sometimes bad.

The days stretched out like a long rubber band, the weather growing colder and colder, the classroom more and more gloomy. Nellie curled up into herself the way she always did, keeping herself safe inside while she sweated and worked and grew afraid of the power these new words had over her, turning her into a different person when she was with Miss Lacey, even if Mrs. Grady and the other teachers saw her the same way.

In Sunday school she had written her rock on a slip of

paper, folded it four times, and slipped it into the box that Mrs. Painter passed around, and she wished hard, squeezing her eyes shut, for honey to flow all at once in a great gush, not in a slow ooze. Waiting was *so* hard!

In the clinic she read *Sam and the Firefly* every day for two weeks once she *could* read it, loving it each time and not wanting to let go, and she was angry when Miss Lacey put it away and made her try a harder book. But then she got sick and was home from school for a week, plus the Thanksgiving vacation.

"Who took my hour, huh? Did you take someone else?" Nellie asked when she came back to school.

Miss Lacey had. "It's like this, Nellie. Some of the children come only once a week, not every day the way you do, so I gave them a little extra time. That's all. No one regular."

Nellie nodded, relieved. "Well, I been thinking of stories . . ."

"About Francina and Melendie?"

"Don't you just know!"

"You've got almost a whole book of those stories by now," Miss Lacey said, adding the last one, "Francina and Melendie Go to a Ball."

"I know! Can I have 'em soon?"

"Soon. First we've got to make up for lost time—Christmas is coming, you know, and I've got some ideas about that!"

About a week before Christmas Mrs. Grady called her up and smiled into her face, "Well, Ellen, I hear you have written a poem. Would you like to read it? I'm sure your classmates would like to hear it."

Nellie wasn't at all certain, but Mrs. Grady didn't give her one minute to say a word. She rapped on her desk. "Class! We'll begin our reading lesson today with a poem that Ellen wrote in her reading clinic. This should make you all work harder!"

Nellie stood in front of the class, without being nervous at all. She was surprised at that. She grinned at them. Some of the boys whistled back. Then she read:

The leaves came down
And down and down.
Red and gold
Yellow and brown.
And then they got mushed
Right into the ground.

The kids clapped for her.

The poem went into her book, too. After that Mrs. Grady did not bother so much with her and she did not bother so much with Mrs. Grady. Old sharp nose. She told Miss Lacey a story about a teacher with a mouth like a ruler and a nose like a pen nib and eyes like finger holes in scissors and teeth like yellow pencils. Boy, did she feel better right then!

And when Miss Lacey explained her idea for a Christmas gift that Nellie could give Mama and Daddy, Nellie rushed so fast into a new story that she had to stop and do it over three times before it all came out just as she wanted it.

THE LITTLE BOY'S SANTA CLAUS

Once there was this little kid who really wanted Santa Claus to come, see, because he didn't know any better. Not that he be dumb or anything like that, only he was little, like my brother Jesse, who just doesn't know much, so he got to get things his own way, Mama says. But one thing sure, he is way out on this Santa Claus bit, only nobody wants to say so. What Jesse wish for more than anything else is this new truck, his old one being all broke up. Every time we go down to the store, Jesse kinda drag along by the hand to make us stop and go back to the drugstore window where the truck is lying, bright red and shiny, begging for us to buy it.

"Ooooh, buy me that," he say, kinda quiet and hopeful but not expecting. And no one say a thing.

Last week Willie, he took Jesse and me to see Santa Claus and I took Francina in my pocket without nobody knowing, and off we went downtown on the bus, just the three of us, not counting Francina, I mean.

Jesse was *so* excited! Me, too. I just stood with
Willie and waited, there was all these people standing
around and lights and trees and toys and this big
Santa Claus. If I didn't know better I'd believe in him,
too, only Willie and me, we just smiled at each
other while Jesse went on up and asked Santa for a
truck and said he been a good boy. Francina
was so excited she almost jumped out of my pocket
and she asked to see Santa 'cause she want a new dress,
silky pink like Grace has got, so I went on up real
close and she whispered into Santa's ear about she
wanting this dress and so's me, all new and silky
pink. Real quiet I say it.

What we all doing in my house, then, is putting our
heads together and some money to buy this truck.
I made thirty-six cents returning bottles for people,
and we added it all up from everyone, Willie and all,
then Sam went out and when he came back, it wasn't
the drugstore truck but one even bigger. I never saw
such a big truck! Daddy be keeping it in the
trunk of his taxi and we all hoping it not get stolen
before Christmas. Mama made a tag saying, "To my
little pal Jesse from Santa."

Now if only I can stop giggling so much when
Jesse see it, Mama says he will keep on believing. And
that's the way it was with this little kid I'm talking
about, only he was all alone and had nobody to give
him a thing. You know, this kid at the beginning. And

he was living way out in the country. And what do you think happened?

Let me think, now.

This farmer, see, came riding by in a mule cart and he had a red hankie sticking from his overalls and a pipe in his mouth and he was going on home for his Christmas dinner which was turkey. And he saw this little kid waiting by the side of the road for Santa Claus, so he took off his hat and he said, "Son, you waiting for Santa Claus?" And the kid, he said, "Yes, sir, I is." And this farmer, he said, "Well, son, you come to the right place to wait, only one thing. I just met Santa Claus not a mile down the road and his sled, it got broke, so he asked me, since I was coming this way, if I would make his apologies to you and give you the things he was hoping to give you himself, namely, this red hankie I just stuck in my pocket and this bag of candy on the seat."

She had ended the story in a rush because she suddenly got lost. Mama had told her stories of back home and Nellie remembered mules and red hankies and no Christmas. But she did not remember any more. Some day she would ask Mama. Some day when she could read her story to Mama and explain it.

Typed up, the story looked beautiful to Nellie. Miss Lacey made a cover of shiny red paper and Nellie drew a picture of a little boy looking like Jesse, and a farmer, and a lopsided Christmas tree, and Francina in her pink dress. Inside she printed "To Mama and Daddy" on one side and "From Nellie" on the other.

She couldn't wait until Christmas Day but only until Daddy came home from work the day she brought it home from school, five days early. Her heart was beating very fast. Daddy leaned back in his chair. "What's this? Minnie, this look something like a gift now, don't it? And since it got a red cover, maybe this be a Christmas gift, what you say?"

Nellie shifted from one foot to another. Daddy passed the book over to Mama.

Mama looked at the cover very carefully, then she opened it slowly, slowly, slowly. "This your work, child?" she asked softly.

"Not the typing, Mama. A teacher did that." Nellie moved closer to Mama and whispered into Mama's soft plump arm.

"You wrote this?" Daddy asked.

"Me. Yes. Yes, I did."

"Why, child . . . !" Mama gave her the biggest hug ever. Daddy gave her a quarter.

"You going to read it to us?" Sam asked.

"Yeah, let's hear it and get it over with," Ramona chimed in.

Nellie swallowed. "I can't really read it, not yet, but soon, you'll see, real soon I can."

"Yah, who ever heard of that? What do you mean?" Sam asked.

"He's right," Grace added. "You trying to fool us, Nellie. You couldn't write that." Grace had been reading the story to herself. "You too dumb to write that!"

"You hush now!" Mama said. "Did you write it, Nellie?" She took Nellie on her knee and looked straight at her with Mama's absolutely no-nonsense-the-Lord-is-watching-you-look.

"I did, Mama, I tell you how. With the magic pencil."

Sam hooted. "You plumb crazy!"

"I'm not! It *is* magic! You don't know—you press a button and talk, then you press another button and all your words come back into the air just like you said them. Like magic. They don't ever go away."

"She means a tape recorder!" Sam said. "Whyn't you say so in the first place?"

Daddy was interested. "What will they think of next? That is really something! So they have got your voice down at school? Well, well!" He opened the newspaper.

Mama beckoned to Nellie. "I moved the truck. Someone would take it out of the trunk, sure as tomorrow morning. Come and see where I put it."

They tiptoed into Willie's room and Mama smiled as she showed Nellie the truck all covered up by a big shirt box she had carefully cut out to fit around the truck.

It was out in plain sight on the shelf, but no one would ever guess it. "Nobody else knows," Mama said, "except Willie, of course, and you and me." She squeezed Nellie's hand.

"And I'm gonna keep your book forever," she said. "So don't let the others fret you. You hear now?"

"Yes, Mama. But, Mama . . ."

"What is it, honey?"

"I *will* read it to you."

"Course you will. Who says otherwise?"

"Mama . . ."

"See, here it go, right in my private drawer under my hankies."

"Mama . . ."

"What's the matter now?"

"I hate Sam."

Mama straightened up. "Hush now! He's the best of all of us! And that be the Lord's own truth. Watch your tongue, girl!"

chapter 10

THE THING WAS, that one story was not enough. Not if Christmas turned out to be one great misery made up of many little miseries. And that was what happened.

It was hard even to figure out just what came first. Emma, maybe. Emma had invited Nellie to bring Francina and come visit her during Christmas, when they could make more doll clothes and divide them up. They talked about it a lot on the telephone and, finally, a day had been set and Mama and Daddy and Gran Rice had all agreed.

Then, the night before, Emma had called to say that she was sick in bed and Nellie couldn't come because of "infection" until after Christmas.

"Sick again?" Nellie asked, angry at Emma for disappointing her.

"Well, I can't help it," Emma said sharply. "Listen, Nell, send me Francina and I'll make clothes for her and Melendie, too. OK? Then when you can come up, everything'll be done."

"But I want to do some of it, too!" Nellie said.

"I don't know how you can without me. You know I make better clothes than you do, Nell."

"Well, I don't want you making clothes for Francina, you makes 'em all too plain. Francina like a little color in what she wear."

"I guess she *does!*" Emma said. "Too much if you ask me."

"I ain't asking you," Nellie shouted. "Right from the start we said I was making clothes for Francina and you was making 'em for Melendie. Not likely I be sending Francina up for you to be spoiling, even if you be sick like you say."

"You are just plain mean, Nell, talking like that," Emma said, sadly.

Nellie denied it, but she knew that Emma was right, at least a little. By the time she finished the telephone call, Nellie did not want to even look at Francina.

That was one thing. Then there was Christmas itself. Sister Painter had a gift for every child in her class—a small New Testament covered in white and an even smaller box of chocolates wrapped in gold paper. She had tied both gifts together with bright red ribbon topped by a big, stiff bow, and it was truly beautiful. Nellie did not even want to open it. But as soon as she got inside the apartment, everyone grabbed for the chocolates and Mama did not say a single word. Nellie did not even have a chance to offer. "Thanks, Nell!" everyone said, but it wasn't the same, not at all. Her gold box was bent and the ribbon cut and there were no marshmallow creams left for her. When she cried and complained, Mama said, "I didn't know Sister Painter was teaching you to be selfish."

"She not!" Nellie could not explain that all she had wanted was the chance to offer the chocolates herself.

"Then don't go 'round sounding like selfish," Mama scolded. By that time the chocolates were gone, anyway.

Nellie got other gifts, too. No pink dress, though. She did get something pink from Willie—a comb and brush and mirror set in pink plastic painted over with pale blue flowers. It was light and gay and cheerful and Nellie loved to look at it. But Ramona and Grace pointed out there was no room on the dresser top for *her* things, so down it went into her drawer where she could hardly see it at all.

Ramona and Grace gave her a thin bracelet with dangling hearts, Mama and Daddy gave a red knitted hood and red mittens, and then, wrapped in two separate little packages of tissue paper and tucked in corners, Nellie found a pair of furry red slippers and a shiny red pocket-book. Now what could be the matter with that? Nothing! Mama and Daddy beamed down at her and she had to smile and thank them; they had spent a lot of money on these gifts, which were useful, besides. If only she had not wanted that dress so much!

Jesse loved his truck and the blocks he got; at least he had something to play with besides the red hat and scarf and mittens Mama and Daddy had bought for him. Sam had gotten a gray sweater and a belt with a shiny buckle, but he seemed dissatisfied, too, so Nellie dared to tell him about the pink dress. Sam just shrugged and said *she* was lucky, he didn't even *know* what *he* wanted.

But none of this was the worst. The worst was the snow that started late on Christmas day and kept right on falling all the next day and night until it was piled up everywhere so that Daddy couldn't even go out in his cab and Mama didn't get home from work until late at night, tired as a clam. And money had to go out— "Wouldn't you know, just after all this Christmas spending," Daddy said, sighing—while not much money was coming in.

Daddy went out shoveling snow for shop owners on their street, walking all the way uptown, working as he went, and coming home with ten dollars, but he didn't like to do this kind of work; it shriveled him up inside, he told Mama, so they all tried to stay quiet and out of his way when he was home.

Willie went to work, no matter what, and Sam

trudged two miles down to the main library, but the rest of them were stuck, waiting until Mama came home all through the long days just to learn that Mama was so tired she didn't want to talk or even to listen, only to get warmed up and go to sleep to get ready for the next day's long bus ride and more work.

Nellie went out twice, running errands for Mrs. Dempster. "Can't get out in this weather, break a leg," she said. "You young now, love the snow, the cold. Me, when I was a kid back in Virginia, the snow came down on the mountains like lace, I had to be out in it, couldn't understand my old folks sitting almost against the fire, like this, all wrapped in quilts. Laughed at 'em. Crazy! Couldn't pay me to venture out now, blood gets cold when you get older. Keep a quarter for yourself this time, child, and send Sam up, I'll give him another list, he can bring me back the heavy stuff. You know what I want, here's a list, can you read it? Coffee, bread, two sticks of margarine, six eggs, milk, couple cans soup, I like 'em all."

"You usually gets plain cookies, too."

"Not this time. Money run out. Neither orange juice."

"I doesn't need the quarter."

"Need it more 'n I need cookies, young as you are. Old folks like me don't need much. Good thing."

By the time vacation was over, Nellie felt like an old lady herself, not needing much, certainly not getting much! Mama never mentioned her book again, not even once, and when Nellie asked about a pink dress, Mama flew at her. "What foolishness am I hearing? No money this week from your Daddy's cab an' such nice things for Christmas an' all! What be getting into you?"

Nellie would show them! She would go back to school and do such wonderful things that everyone would have to give her just what she wanted! For the first time ever, she looked forward to that first day of school in the new year. But then it snowed again and they were wet and cold by the time they got into the steamy building and Nellie almost didn't remember why she was pleased to be back until she went down to the clinic after lunch and it was dark, the door was locked, and there was a note on the door, "Miss Lacey will be here on Tuesday."

Nellie was too mad to cry. She was so mad she didn't know what to do with all that anger. After school she picked a fight with Leroy Clagget and got hit with a dozen snowballs, but she landed one good hard ice ball smack on his face and then she felt a little bit better, even though she knew she would get scolded for being wet from top to toe.

On Tuesday, Nellie half expected the clinic to be locked again, but it wasn't. She slammed the door behind her when she came into the room.

Miss Lacey was filling out some forms and looked tired. "Quiet with that door! Oh, hi, Nellie. Just wait a sec, will you? Have to finish these papers, or I'll go crazy. I've never seen such a bad start to a new year."

"*Wait!*" All of Nellie's old anger came back, sour-tasting and disagreeable. "That's *all* I been doing. You wasn't here yesterday; I came down an' you wasn't here. You s'pozed to be here an' you wasn't! My Daddy, he say teachers get lots of money, *some* of 'em doing lots of nothing, like Miz Grady. You just like Miz Grady an' I hate you!"

Nellie was astonished to hear herself saying that; she didn't *mean* to say it. The words just came out of her mouth and there they were. It was the snow she hated and the miserable vacation, but never Miss Lacey.

Miss Lacey looked up from the desk and stared at Nellie until Nellie dropped her eyes to the floor. "You've got a few things to learn, little miss! For one thing, the snow ruined the flight schedules from Chicago and I sat up all Sunday night in the terminal just so I could get back in time for today. For another, you just go and march right up to your class and let me call *you* next time I want to see you. Now, go on, go on! You've said enough!"

Nellie found herself in the hall, still mad, but scared, too. The door closed firmly behind her. She hid out in the girls' bathroom for the rest of the hour.

A whole week went by. Nellie waited for a note to come to Mrs. Grady. Nothing came. She snuck into the girls' bathroom every day, wishing Miss Lacey would say something. Oh, she wanted to go back! But she was scared. Maybe Miss Lacey wouldn't let her finish up her book *By Nellie Cameron* and take it with her to show Mama and Daddy. She missed seeing the way that book got thicker every day. All she had was the Christmas booklet Mama had put away.

Nellie slipped it out of Mama's drawer and put it under her own pillow. What a beautiful story! Every night after she went to bed but before Grace and Ramona came in, she would sit up cross-legged holding that story in her lap and squinting at the words as she tried to read them. The lamp on the dresser cast a weak light on the pages. It seemed to her that each word shone golden.

The first night she struggled without making any sense out of the marks on the paper. She knew she had said words. They were bouncing around in her head. But where did they go on the page? She felt that her head would burst from trying. But it didn't burst. Only a few words said anything at all.

Strangely, the next time she could make out more words. Maybe sleeping on the story pushed those words into her head! She looked at it with more admiration each time she studied it. She could not stay away from that story. Each time she looked at it, she felt bigger.

So on Thursday she took it to school with her, like a charm. She was sure she even looked taller, trudging through the snow and slush with Sam and crying Jesse. She even forgot to be careful; she forgot all Mama's warnings about never letting anybody know anything about your very own self.

It was so cold that the school was open early and they could all go into the assembly room to wait for the bell. Nellie looked around the room. LaVerne was not there. She was not surprised. LaVerne had no real winter coat, no stockings, and no heavy shoes, so of course she would not be in school on such a cold day.

Nellie unpeeled her own layers of clothing, from Grace's old coat to Sam's old sweater to her own old sweater, and finally she was down to her old cotton dress that Mama had starched so that it stood out stiffly all around. She smoothed out her new hat and scarf and mittens. The bright red color was cheerful now that she was used to it.

Then she sighed. All around her the room was full of noise and motion, boys and girls moving up and down the aisles and talking, some kids eating chocolate bars or peanuts out of crunchy bags, a lot of boys pitching pennies. Sam wasn't there. He worked for Mrs. Harper, the kindergarten teacher, fixing up the room and getting things ready for the little kids. The Morgan boys, Bennie and Billie, were playing harmonicas in one corner; they were going to have a band as soon as they got older. Other girls were playing jacks, but nobody stopped for Nellie to join in.

She sighed again and opened her booklet. All the words she had learned last night had gotten lost again!

The shapes danced around on the page and she couldn't pin them down to look at them. The old panic slipped through her, from her stomach to her feet and hands.

"Hey! Ain't you getting good now!"

Nellie jumped.

"Whatcha doing, teeny?"

It was Leroy Clagget, with one big fat hand heavy on her shoulder.

"You leave me alone, Leroy! Go on now!"

"You gonna make me? Hah!"

"I'll tell the teacher on you, Leroy!"

"Oh, I'm scairt of that, I am! You too dumb to think of anything better than that, ain't ya?"

"Shut up, you Leroy! You just don't know one single thing, you don't! You the one dumb. What I'm doing is reading my very own story, one I made up myself, just like a real book."

"Liar, liar, Nellie is a liar!" Leroy chanted right in her ear and to the rest of the room.

Miss Beach looked up wearily. "That you again, Leroy? Can't you ever be still? Come on over next to me and sit down, why don't you? The bell will ring in a minute. I guess you can manage a minute of quiet."

On the way out of the assembly room Leroy pulled one of Nellie's braids and when she turned around, he made a face at her.

"Dumb!" she hissed.

"Liar!" Nothing would stop that Leroy.

At lunchtime they could go out, into the glittering sunshine of the bright winter day that had risen from the slush and gloom of that morning. The sun struck glints off the windows and made them look like diamonds. When Nellie drew a deep breath, her throat and lungs ached. Still, she drew many deep breaths, for the cold, effortless air was pure and seemed to be as shining as the sun.

The boys and girls ran together in the cold, chasing and running and hiding. Their books lay in untidy heaps at the fringes of the yard because they could not safely leave them in a building without lockers. Things were stolen right out in the open, too, but it was easier for the teachers on duty to watch children straying too close to the books. Every minute whistles blew shrilly into the clear air.

Two sharp blasts from Mr. Truesdale's whistle meant "Get your books! On the double!" Everyone ran toward the book piles, falling, pushing, shoving, and laughing. The big kids made a mess of everything while the little kids cried. No one seemed to care.

"Get away from my things, Leroy! An' stay away!" Nellie cried out, scrambling for her things. Her books and papers were in a nice mess!

"See you after your reading work!" Orinda called, flying away over the playground.

Nellie did not even answer. She gathered her things together as best she could and walked slowly into the building, waiting until the other children were in class, then ducking into the girls' bathroom where she could get her breath back and sort out her papers. They were usually messy enough without any help from Leroy Clagget. Who put him on earth just to bother her anyway?

Sitting on the damp cement floor she stuck her papers back into her notebook, then slipped the damp book covers back on her reading book and her speller. Only when she had gotten down to the bottom of the pile of papers did she realize that something was missing. Her Christmas story! Frantically this time, she turned the pages of her notebook; maybe she had put the story in it by mistake. She looked again. She got up and searched every place on the floor but it wasn't there. She did not dare go out into the hall until the period was over.

The book was gone. She sat down against a peeling wall and hugged her knees to her chest for whatever comfort they gave. She listened to the water dripping from a leaky faucet. She smelled the sickly disinfectant smell. She heard the beat of her heart. And there came over her a terrible feeling, worse than anything she had ever known before, a feeling of being all alone, almost without herself, just a shadow of a girl who was suddenly a stranger. Miss Lacey did not want her back. She could not tell Mama because she had taken Mama's book without asking, and how could she explain the emptiness that had made her take it when the emptiness she felt right now was a million times greater? The book had been so beautiful! And now it was gone. She was sweating in that cold room, yet there were goose bumps on her skin.

What she wanted to do was plain sit in that dirty corner the rest of her life, but she was afraid to do that. When the bell rang chattering girls would come rushing in, their pointing fingers would pick her out, and she would be worse off than ever. Hating them bitterly, she gathered the books that meant nothing to her, and scuffled off to her class just in time, keeping her eyes down on the floor and not saying a word to anyone. All the rest of the afternoon, she sat at her desk, miserable.

At three o'clock there was that Leroy Clagget again, bumping into her. Just one more awful thing.

"Nellie, guess what I got?" he said, sneering and grinning all together. "Your book, that what! Your special book! Only it ain't so special, *I* says! I going to rip it up!" And he danced away from her, squirming through the crowds of children.

"You give that back!" Nellie screamed, chasing after him. Tears ran down her cheeks and almost blinded her, pouring so fast out of her eyes. "Give it back!"

Leroy raced on, looking behind him and laughing, still waving the book high above his head. An awful wail of grief and anger escaped from Nellie's mouth. She was surprised at it herself. She had no idea such a sound was in her. "It's mine!" she howled.

At that awful sound Leroy stopped. Sam came running up to her to ask what was the matter, was she sick or something, and all she could do was point wordlessly to where Leroy stood, waving her book back and forth in the air.

Sam pulled her along with him. "One thing after another," he grumbled.

"But . . . my book . . ." Nellie finally managed to sob.

Sam turned to face the other boy. "OK, Leroy, hand it over. Making a holy show of yourself, too!"

"What you going to give me, wise guy?" Leroy and Sam were sort of friends; they played basketball together at the Boy's Club and talked about Elgin Baylor and Lew Alcindor being *cool.* So Leroy just stood there dancing around a little, not running away.

"A beating," Sam answered with considerable satisfaction. "You've caused too much trouble already. Don't you know when to stop?"

Leroy's arm buckled slightly. Sam reached over, whipped the book out of his hand, and handed it to Nellie. "OK, here's your stuff, Nellie, and you can stop crying, or someone'll think you are in *real* trouble."

Nellie looked at him, astonished. "But I *was* in real trouble! This book . . . it's mine, Sam. I mean, *I* did it. It's my own words."

Sam looked down at her. Nellie was suddenly aware

of how much taller than she Sam was; he looked *way* down.

"OK, then it's important," Sam said. "I'm glad I could get it back. Only listen, Nell, don't mess around with that Leroy anymore!"

But Nellie was no longer listening. All the way home she kept turning the pages of her story, remembering what she had said in it, and being thrilled all over again.

chapter 11

NEXT DAY AFTER LUNCH Nellie didn't stop to think. She moved. She knocked on Miss Lacey's door, opened it and walked right in. She didn't look down at her feet this time! She looked straight at Miss Lacey and said, "I'm sorry." Then she took off her coat and showed Miss Lacey where her Christmas book had been crumpled. "Leroy Clagget did it. Know him?"

"Should I?"

"Nah. I guess he can do his work OK, but he is the meanest! Well, he grabbed my book and said it wasn't mine and it *was* mine!"

Miss Lacey smiled. "That is about the longest sentence I have ever heard you say, do you know that?"

"Can you fix it?" Nellie asked. "I took it from my Mama."

"Why not? Let me write a note first—do you know what I've been doing during *your* hour, as you call it? Testing some junior primary kids for promotion. Here, take this note to Miss Dove—*if* you don't mind, Miss Pepper!"

When Nellie came back they worked together on a new cover of shiny red paper.

Then Miss Lacey said thoughtfully, "You know, Nellie, any book you can read is yours in a way. It belongs to you in a *special* way. Never mind how anyone else feels about it. Nobody can take *your* book away from you. The words are right there in your head."

Nellie giggled. "Like your sins," she said, thinking of Preacher Evans, who used almost the same words. "They yours for all time, seems like."

"And your mistakes," Miss Lacey said grimly. Then her face changed suddenly, the way the sun will cast its light across the shape of rain clouds, and she laughed. Nellie had not heard such bright laughter from her. "You can't have so many sins now, can you?"

Nellie hesitated. She rolled her eyes. "I been born again in the Lord," she said, and giggled. "My Mama, she looooves the church."

"My Mama was the same. For me . . ."

"I didn't usta care. Except for the singing. Now we

got this teacher and she's something else, I don't know exactly how to say, but now I like to go. Her words . . . ummm . . ." Nellie shrugged helplessly and waved her arms. "Last week we was learning from the Psalms like every week and we got to learn 'The sparrow has found its home at last, the swallow a nest for its young, your altars, My Lord, my king and my God.' " Nellie grinned. "It sure is pretty."

Miss Lacey sat quietly for a minute. "Yes. It certainly is." Then she drew a sheet of white paper out of a drawer. "Why don't you write your verses down every week for your book? Let me print that verse out, and you can copy it."

Nellie printed as carefully as she could. No more scrawls. She really wanted the page to look nice. How bold the black letters looked against the creamy white smoothness of the paper! Doing this, she felt the two good halves of her life joining together to make a whole, a circle. And she was in the center of this circle. It felt wonderfully good.

"There!"

"When you have some time, you can paint in a border. I'll show you how, later on. I guess you'd better get back to work now, though." Miss Lacey sounded sad again and looked absorbed. Nellie could tell she wasn't going to talk anymore.

Nellie found this new book much easier. It did not have big pictures and only a few words on the page.

This book had some pictures but more words lined up one after the other. Some pages had no pictures at all! She liked them the best of all. They looked neat and trim with their black-and-white lines marching from side to side, from top to bottom. A couple of times she grew hot and clammy and her stomach was sick as she strained to read, word-by-word, line-by-line, but Miss Lacey said nothing. Miss Lacey did not stop her and call her stupid. She just leaned back and waited. She seemed to have all the time in the world.

They worked the same way every day now. Book followed book. Good days came after bad days. Bad days were fewer. Sometimes Nellie was scared, but not so much. Her own book grew and so did the list of books she could read.

Still, at home she said hardly a word. "Oh, sure, fine, all right," she mumbled, turning away. "Real good this year."

Her winter report card did not list one F! After Daddy signed it, he and Mama talked together for a long time. Then Mama said, "Honey, whyn't you get your jar?"

When they counted the dimes in neat piles on the table, there were four dollars. Then Daddy did something Nellie had never seen. He took out four dollars of his own and put them down next to the dimes. She had never known anyone to get four dollars all at once before, not even Sam.

Mama patted her hand. "Let me keep this until Saturday, chick. Then, oh my, well, whyn't you wait and see? We gonna have some fun!"

That was enough for now. Nellie did not need to say more. What could she add to that report card? And the whole eight dollars!

By the time Saturday came around Willie had given her another dollar. Mama said, "Big surprise for Nellie!" to Jesse, and off they went, just the two of them, down the street to the shops.

"What we getting?" Nellie asked.

"Hush now, and you'll see!" Mama was having even a better time than Nellie. There was such a good feeling between them! They kept squeezing hands, and Mama walked lightly, like a girl, for all her size. Had Mama cared so much then?

"Here we be," Mama said, standing underneath a gay red-and-white-striped awning.

It was a shoe store!

"For me, Mama?"

"Who else? It's your money. I'd say you done earned it."

When the salesman came, Mama said, "Shoes for the young lady."

"And we got nine dollars to spend, too!" Nellie said.

"Have you now? You sure get a good pair of shoes for nine dollars!"

The salesman brought back a big stack of boxes. Inside

them were red shoes, blue shoes, shiny black shoes, brown shoes, and white. There were shoes with laces, buckles, and straps.

"Oh no, missy, you decide," Mama declared when Nellie asked for help. "Go ahead!"

Truth was, Nellie liked the shiny black shoes with a strap the best. But they were clearly only for best, and she wanted shoes of her own to wear for every day. No more penny loafers, that she knew!

The salesman went off to wait on other people and left them alone. Nellie was dizzy with thinking. "Oooh, Mama!"

"Now, brown-and-white's awful hard to keep clean."

"These brown look kinda common."

Mama considered. "Black goes with everything. Even spring things."

"Navy blue's nice. Why, I bet no one at school has blue shoes!"

"They can polish up real good, too."

Finally, Nellie was down to red ghillies with red-and-black-checked laces, and blue shoes with a wide strap and a gold side buckle. She tried one pair on. Then the other.

The salesman came back to them. "Made up your mind yet?"

Suddenly, she had. "The blue, please."

"Wear 'em out?"

"Oh no! I'm gonna save 'em for Sunday first!"

They cost eight dollars and seventy-nine cents with the tax. Mama bought some wax polish for her, too, and the salesman gave her a balloon and a comic book. "Can I have a balloon for my baby brother?"

"Why not?" He gave her a handful, all colors. Red, yellow, green, blue, and white balloons.

"Mama, know what?" Nellie asked as they were walking home, faster now, because Mama had so much to do. "This is the best day in my whole life!"

"That so? Ain't that nice!" And Mama threw back her head and laughed for sheer joy.

chapter 12

TIME AND AGAIN that spring Mama said it was a good thing they had bought Nellie those shoes, for money was tight again. Worse than ever.

One day Willie walked in from work with a girl. Willie had always gone his own way since he had finished high school and gotten a job; to Nellie he seemed more like Daddy than like an older brother, so remote was he in the grown-up world. He had his friends and his girls; sometimes the children met him hanging around the Soul Shack, but by and large he went his own slow, quiet way. Last year he had taken all of them to the circus and at times he surprised them with a record or tickets to the Booker T. for a good variety show, but once he paid his board to Mama, the rest of his money belonged to him and made him freer than the others.

But this girl was different. "Meet Donice," Willie said. "We going to marry at the end of June. After school's out. Donice's sister be graduating from high school, then she can work an' Donice be free to marry."

Willie never talked much. Donice didn't talk much, either, but what she said, you knew she was a girl with her own mind. Yes, she belonged to a church, she told Mama. Elder Michaux's church. Everyone could tell that Mama was satisfied at that! Willie had met her at work. He was a garage mechanic and she was cashier in the office.

"She has been to business school after high school," Willie said proudly, and they all looked at Donice. Nellie thought she looked like a picture from a magazine with her smooth black hair and the make-up all around her eyes. Grace would have plenty to learn from *her!*

"You makes a handsome couple," Daddy said.

"She want the best," Willie added.

"She think you the best, son?" Mama asked, joking. "Guess I got to agree. You a girl with real taste, Donice," Mama said. "Welcome to our family."

Willie didn't give money at home anymore now that he was saving for his own place. Every weekend he and Donice looked at apartments. Rents were high.

"You got big ideas, you got to pay for 'em," Daddy said. "Little place not good enough for you."

"No," said Willie, "nor for Donice. Only the best good enough for us."

"Good luck," said Daddy.

Without Willie's money things were tight. On top of that, Mama and Daddy started saving to buy Willie what he most wanted, a stereo and television set all in one. Every week they put some dollars on it in the store. Seemed like with one thing and another there was never enough money to go around, no matter what. But Nellie had her shoes!

She rubbed them with a cloth every night and put them under her pillow when she went to sleep. Who cared? No one! Grace smiled when she noticed. Ramona didn't even see the shoes. Ramona was always jawing, jawing, jawing. One of her teachers found her a summer job so she'd stay in school. From the way Ramona went on about it, you'd think no one ever had such a job before. Oh, she made a big thing out of it! She would be taking care of the kids for some fancy family at Rehoboth Beach.

"Why, you'll be nothing but a maid!" Grace said.

"Ha! That's all you know! I be taking care of the children alone. Mrs. Purdy said I'd be a governess and learning about children an' all. Mrs. Purdy, she said maybe I could get to be a child nurse if I kept on in school, just from this job."

"Well, good luck to you!" Grace said nastily. But she had nothing more to add. Ramona would be making thirty dollars a week plus her room and board. She was going to spend every cent of it on clothes when she came home in the fall.

What Mama decided was she would get a sewing machine. They would pay it out two dollars a week, and that way Ramona's money would go a lot further and Mama could make Grace some clothes besides. Grace would be starting high school in September, and she was determined to get away from her old skirts and blouses at last.

Mama started by making summer clothes for them all. Her face was tired and crumpled up with worry, all the time trying to figure out how she was to pay for the machine and the material for clothes when less money was coming in and more, it seemed, going out.

"You be having nice clothes soon, too, Nellie girl," Mama assured her. But Nellie hadn't seen any yet. The clatter of the sewing machine racketed in her head. How could she do her homework with so much noise? She was losing ground again and dreaded the spring report card. Mrs. Grady said nothing about taking her away from Miss Lacey's clinic but she never asked to hear Nellie read anymore or even go to the board for arithmetic.

One warm night in April Mama came home panting. "What kind of a summer is we going to have with such a day this time of the year?"

Daddy looked up from his soup. "Hot," he said, winking at Nellie. "Good growing weather."

"Pity we not corn," Mama said. "But we not. Seems to me it get hotter and hotter."

"Summer is as God made it, Minnie."

"Don't you go teasing me now, Eli Cameron. You know 'zactly what I mean. What we going to do with these kids in the summer?" She pointed across the table. "Ramona, now that's fine. Willie be out of here. Truth is, I don't see Grace spending no summer cooped up here watching the little ones. No, sir, I don't see it at all."

"Church doing anything?"

Mama dipped her spoon in the soup and out again. "Two weeks' camp. You know they got no money, Eli."

"Well, don't look at me, woman! I got the same kind of no money the church got."

"It worries my mind to think I be working every day and they here home alone. Don't see my way to doing that. And that Mrs. Barker, my Monday and Thursday lady, she talking about raising me three dollars a week plus another three if I stay on Thursday and make supper for them all. Can't see myself saying no to that. Six dollars . . ."

"Course you won't listen to my ideas, Minnie, but I do get one every now and then, and I got one now," Daddy said. "Whyn't we send 'em on down to Gar and Tillie? What it cost you to feed the four of 'em each week? Send Gar and Tillie twenty dollars a week for the lot of them—why, I bet they'll put money away on that and feed 'em better than we do here! Just think of the garden they put in! Gar'll take Sam fishing; I guess they be doing right well."

"Can we go, Mama?" Nellie asked. "Can we really go?"

"You *wants* to go? No end to surprises! I don't know, Eli. Times is changing so . . . they not brought up in the South, how they gonna manage?" Her voice was tight.

"Gar an' Tillie, they manage themselves, don't they? You worry too much, Minnie. They just kids."

Mama shrugged. "Jesse, maybe. Nellie even. But Sam? He too smart. Grace, I think she can work at the two weeks' camp for the church, that run six weeks taking three groups of chil'rens. I go talk to Sister Ellis, I think she say *yes* to that. Gracie, she be good with chil'rens, she full of ideas."

Daddy grinned. "See? I'm getting 'em settled already!"

They had rice pudding for dessert. Nellie picked out all the raisins and gave them to Jesse.

"You crazy, sister," he said, gulping them down. "Thanks."

"Well, if I'm crazy, it's a good thing for you, raisin-pig."

"Those two do right well together," Mama said. "Maybe you right, Eli. I'll write Tillie after supper, see what she think. Five dollars a week for each, you think?"

"That just about right, seem to me," Daddy said. "Hey, who made this rice pudding?"

"Me," Ramona said.

"It surprisingly good, girl. You getting like your Mama. I'm glad to see it." Daddy got the scrapings from the dish. "So you all settled, Nellie, you and Jesse. Off to the country. My, my! Now we gots to put our minds to Sam here."

Sam cut right in. "Don't you worry about me. I can take care of myself." The way he said it, so certain, surprised them all into silence.

But he said no more and still had not come forth with his plans by the time the letter came from South Carolina. Mama read it out one night after supper. "Dearest Sister and Brother. Hope you are keeping well one and all. Things are well here, God be praised. Thankful you are keeping in touch. Tillie joins me in saying it would be our pleasure to take the children for all the time you wish. The sum you write would be good, dear Sister. We do love to see the children of our dear Sister and Brother. We will put in a garden for them. It is lonely here without Cindy and Jacky and Solomon. Praise God they are well. Dinah and Allie welcome their Cousins too. Your loving Brother Garwood."

Mama folded the letter. "Well, I guess that do settle it. How we get 'em there, Eli?"

"I know a man is a porter on a Seaboard Pullman. Let me see what he can do."

On the train! Most of the people Nellie knew went by bus from the dirty bus station downtown. But the train! And all by themselves! "When we coming back, Mama?"

Mama was not really listening. Nellie could tell from the look on her face that she was adding money up in her head. "Hmm? All summer, whyever not?"

"But my birthday, Mama! I be having my birthday in August!"

Jesse began to cry, following Nellie. "Oooh, Mama, I don't want to go!"

Mama looked mad. "Never heard such foolishness!"

"But my birthday . . ."

"Enough!" Mama said. "Think Gar an' Tillie won't be giving you a birthday? Dinah an' Allie, too, your cousins an' all. Maybe you be having a picnic. What you think going to happen, child? This place be my *home*, your Daddy's, too."

Then Mama did something unlike her. She leaned back in her chair, and let her hand drop loosely without being busy with anything. "Come here, chil'ren, you come right here. I'm going to tell you a story 'cause you know I growed up right in that same place. New house, though, bigger house, better house, yes, sir, but the very same land I growed up on, so I am the one to tell you.

What do you want to hear first? The house? Or the land?"

Jesse stopped sniffling. Nellie said, "Oh, the house, the house!"

"It looks like a little-bitty house but it kinda grows when you gets to know it. There be a good front porch high up. You sits out in a rocking chair and you sees the whole front yard all blooming and blossoming with flowers.

"Then there's a big front room, fixed up real nice, for company and for sitting in the winter. I guess you won't be in there much. 'Cause there's a big kitchen—you eat there—and next to that a screened porch in the back, that's where you sleep in the summer. And the room for Uncle Gar and Aunt Tillie you won't be seeing much, but it's there next the porch."

Mama stopped talking. She was thinking. A little smile flickered on her face.

"Gar earned the lumber for that porch and the upstairs. And when it was built, he painted the whole house white. Only house thereabouts painted. That white!" Mama sketched in the air with her hand. "Wisht I could tell you what it looked like, all white and shining. And Tillie's red geraniums all around. And the green woods behind it. I tell you, it was a house! Don't know as I've seen a thing prettier. Long time ago . . ."

Daddy reached over and patted her hand. "Twenty-five years, Minnie," he said. "About as long as we been married."

Mama nodded. "Some ways a long time. Some ways it not seem so long, Eli."

She paused. Finally, Nellie asked, "What about the land?"

"That? Well, you get fresh vegetables all summer from the garden. There's a creek for fishing and swimming. A big old pecan tree to climb. And there's nuts, and blackberries, all you want."

"One thing you forgot," Daddy put in. "They gots a dog, Roswell's dog I guess it is, but he too old for a dog to play with, he only use it for hunting."

Jesse jumped up and down, he was so excited. "What kind a dog? What's his name? Is he big?"

"Oh, I guess he be right big, son. Maxey, a coon hound. Yes, a big dog, sure enough." Daddy chuckled.

Mama got up. "No use talking anymore. It decided. Ramona, you and Grace do the dishes. I'm on my way to see Sister Morris and Sister Painter to pray on it."

Before she went to sleep Nellie imagined the black fields and blue sky, the hot sun baking her, the cold water pumped from the well, the joy of being outside— with Maxey—instead of staying in the hot apartment. When she saw herself tasting the good food Mama talked about, her mouth watered.

And then it went dry. Mama and Daddy's words had been soft and sweet; Nellie could tell how much they liked that old place. But there was a shadow on those words, too, a shadow of loss and going away and emptiness—the same feeling she had known when her Christmas booklet was missing. Something special had gone. Only for Mama and Daddy it would not be found again.

"I'm scairt to go," Nellie whispered when Mama dropped in to say good night.

Mama just said, "Hush," and patted her head, but on top of and around Nellie's scared feeling because she would be going to a strange place, came a new, good feeling.

Maybe she would find a special something back there in South Carolina, the way she had found her book.

chapter 13

NOW THAT THEY WERE ALL taken care of for the summer except Sam, Mama and Daddy turned their mind to him, but without pushing too much. Sam had changed, almost right before their eyes. He didn't fight with them very much and his old sullenness was gone. So was most of his teasing and laughter. He seemed to have curled up into himself and lived in the house like a soft-footed ghost.

"Feeling sickly, son?"

"You wouldn't understand, Mama, believe me," Sam said wearily.

"They making you work too hard in school?"

Sam hooted. "*That* school? No, Mama. It's like this . . . I'm doing special work, I want to do it."

Mama shook her head. "Don't seem right, you working so hard when you so smart. Sure no one treating you wrong?"

"Mama, I said I can take care of myself," Sam said abruptly, in a way that put an end to the conversation.

Mama and Daddy tried once or twice more, but Sam would not tell them anything except not to worry about him. Everyone was so busy thinking about Willie's wedding and getting ready to send Nellie and Jesse to South Carolina, that two weeks went by in a bustle of sewing, making lists, and talking about what was coming, not what was plain in front of them. Then Sam brought a note home from school saying that Mr. Wallace, the school principal, would like to call on them in person that very night if it was convenient.

The principal! To Nellie he seemed about twelve feet high with a voice like a drum and a hand like a paddle, and she did not even like to go past his office.

That evening, after supper, they all waited for Mr. Wallace in the front room, Daddy in his chair and Mama in one corner of the sofa. Nellie sat in the creaky rocking chair, trying very hard to keep from banging it against the floor. Sam had brought his desk chair from his room and sat very straight in it, a little apart from the rest of them. At the last minute Jesse squeezed in next to Nellie. Grace and Ramona stood in the shadows near the door to the hall, hoping they would not be noticed.

Daddy warned Nellie and Jesse, "You sit quietly now, or out you go!"

"Yes, sir," they each nodded in turn. Nellie wanted to hide when Mr. Wallace walked up their stairs but she didn't dare move, just sat with her eyes on the flowered rug until everything began to look double, and she blinked. Then she looked up.

Mr. Wallace didn't appear much taller than Daddy! And his voice was quiet. "Mr. Cameron. Mrs. Cameron." He shook hands. Mama kept brushing her damp palms down against her best church dress. Only Daddy looked calm, his usual smile decorating his face. Nellie loved that face. It was always the same, nothing would ever surprise it.

"It is your son, Sam, I wish to talk about. May I?" Mr. Wallace sat down at the other end of the sofa, right at home.

"Some coffee?" Mama's voice was throaty.

"Why, thank you." And Mr. Wallace took some of Grace's cookies. "I trust you realize what a remarkable boy you have. Not that there isn't room for improvement now and then, ha-ha!"

Oh, Nellie knew a thing or two about that Sam, but of course she kept herself quiet, looking and listening but not saying one single word.

"Nevertheless, I may say that he is our star student, our prize pupil." He nodded at Sam. "That boy will go far."

"Yes, sir," Mama whispered.

Daddy took some coffee and settled back in his chair.

"Specifically I am here for your signature on these approval forms. However, there is more to it than a mere signature."

Daddy rolled his eyes. Mama glared at him. Nellie giggled behind her hand. Daddy meant: when is he going to stop talking and say something?

Finally Mr. Wallace said it. Sam had taken a special exam at school and he had won. "This exam makes Sam eligible for a scholarship to one of the best boarding schools in the country. Yes, one of the best. And there is no question that he deserves it."

Nellie's mouth dropped open. A scholarship! And Sam had not said a word to any of them.

Mr. Wallace wiped his mouth carefully and put the coffee cup down. Mama's eyes never left his face. Daddy lit a cigar. Mama glared at him worse than ever, then she stared at Mr. Wallace again.

"Cigar, Mr. Wallace?"

"Thank you. I do like a cigar now and again." Mr. Wallace drew on it and a tiny flame hissed. "Very good."

He puffed a few times before going on. "To make a long story short, a Mr. Herbert Wylie saw Sam for about two hours today in my office. Afterwards, Mr. Wylie, a very busy man indeed, took the trouble to advise me that he will recommend a full scholarship for Sam at the Clarke School in September. Let me tell you that this is a considerable sum—in the vicinity, I believe, of . . . ahem . . . four thousand dollars for tuition, room and board, each year."

Daddy finally spoke. "Four thousand dollars?" he asked, as if he were choking.

"That is correct. And this will continue for each of the six years if Sam maintains his marks."

"What is this Clarke School?" Mama asked.

"It is one of the five or six best boys' schools in the country, an old school. It accepts very few black students, very few. It is in New Hampshire and Sam would live there during the school year except for holidays. There is no finer education available for a gifted boy anywhere."

"Sam?" Mama croaked, before she lost her voice altogether.

"Well, well . . ." Daddy began. He looked hard at Sam, who looked straight back.

Mr. Wallace smiled a thin ribbon of a smile. "Mr. Wylie went on to add that he personally was so impressed by Sam's obvious ability and maturity that he would like to make an . . . additional gift of a scholarship to a summer camp in New Hampshire connected with the Clarke School. Sam would not only have all the usual amenities of a camper—swimming, boating, and so on—but he would be tutored every day in those subjects he will be studying next year—French, geometry, biology, and so on. Right, Sam?"

Sam nodded.

"I had no idea," Daddy was saying, "that Sam could do this. I knew he was doing well, but this . . ." There was a long silence.

Mr. Wallace coughed. "Well, Mr. Cameron, that's about it. The only thing that remains to be done is for you to sign these." He handed him the approval forms.

"Yes, of course. If you'll just leave 'em here, so I can take a good look at 'em when all's quiet, I'd appreciate it."

Daddy did not say *sir* to Mr. Wallace, Nellie noticed. Once Daddy had told them that he had gotten so tired saying *sir* to every white man that passed his way, he had run out of *sirs* and wasn't going to say it anymore to anyone. Nellie kept listening, but Daddy was true to his word.

Mr. Wallace shook hands with Daddy and Mama and patted Sam on the shoulder. Then he caught sight of the rest of them. "Evening, Ellen. When are we going to hear good things about you? You must be inspired by your brother. Yes, inspired."

Nellie shook so hard she had to lean against the wall. "Yes, sir."

Mr. Wallace went on down the stairs.

Mama and Daddy weren't even thinking of putting the children to bed. Ramona took Jesse away but Nellie just sat.

"Whyn't you say anything, son?" Mama asked Sam. Daddy was reading the forms and mumbling, "My, my!" as he read.

"How can you ask me that?" Sam cried. "Any time I try to say anything, you tell me: be a good boy, son, listen to the teachers, keep your mouth shut, don't let anyone know what you are thinking. That's *your* way. Anyway, I want to go, but other than that there's nothing I *can* say!"

Daddy looked up. "Sam, don't talk like that to your Mama. She do her best for you."

"I don't aim to be fresh—oh, you don't understand, either!"

"You going to handle yourself so far away in a white school?" Daddy asked quietly.

"Don't know," Sam admitted, cooling down. "I'm going to try. Won't any of those kids be as tough as me . . ."

"Maybe not. But tough ain't all."

Sam nodded. "Couldn't be worse than here, the school, I mean. Nothing could," he added bleakly.

"I just don't understand, son," Mama murmured. "Don't know what to say, only pray to the Lord."

"Oh, Mama, I don't need prayers!"

"Thinking you don't is when you need 'em most," Mama insisted.

"You let your Mama pray for you, son," Daddy ordered in his quiet way. "You going to need a lot of help, no matter what you be thinking. Some things you *don't* know, you'll find out. You kinda young, no matter what. I'll sign your forms, see you going away, but you always gots a home here, place to come back to, your own folks all around. Only one thing I gots to say, son— don't forget who you is. No one else ever let you forget, that one thing for sure!"

"Second thing for sure," Mama said, "we be proud of you." And Daddy nodded.

Nellie had never hated anyone as much as she hated Sam then. She would never bring her books home and read to them, she would never let them know. Never! Never would they look at her as they did at Sam, with love spilling from their eyes, and pride and a little fright. And oh, she wanted it!

She ran to her room and cried so hard Mama thought she was having a fit.

"She just jealous," Ramona said, giggling. And Nellie kicked her.

"Enough of that!" Mama said sharply to both of them. "All right, Nellie, stop that crying now. Here's some coffee and milk for you."

While Nellie sat up and drank the coffee, Mama sponged her face down. "Guess all of us got something to be jealous of," Mama admitted. "Ain't it so, Ramona?"

"Huh! I ain't jealous," Ramona said.

"Maybe you should be," Mama said mildly. "Just a little, enough to do some schoolwork of your own."

Nellie caught her breath. "I be doing good work, Mama," she whispered.

"I know you are, honey, I felt it," Mama said. "I ain't worried about *you*, none. But Sam, he worry me, you understand?"

Nellie nodded and smiled but the hard lump of hate settled firmly in her stomach.

chapter 14

MISS LACEY LOOKED NARROWLY at her. "Well, out with it!"

Nellie stared open-eyed. "Ma'am? You want me to try again?" She bent to the words. "During the morn . . . morning, Ida con . . . con . . . I'll skip that one . . . what to do. She knew she had a prob . . . prob . . ." Her voice faded.

"We going to call all this time a *waste?*"

Nellie admired her shoes. "No, ma'am."

Miss Lacey reached over and clapped the book shut. Nellie had nothing to fiddle with.

"Have some coffee. Go ahead. And some cookies if you want." Miss Lacey was used to waiting. She prepared herself to wait.

Nellie thought for a minute. She tried to get the words in the right order before she spoke them. No one had a right to know her private self. Mama insisted on that. Even her new shoes had gotten old and messed up from wearing them; what would happen to her own self if she took it out too often? But right next to her private self there was another self she could let out to view. That would keep people from asking further questions and she would be safe where it counted.

"Well," she began, "you said everyone would care when they found out that I was reading. And it don't make no difference, none at all! Not with Sam around!" Hesitating over what to say, Nellie told Miss Lacey a little about Sam.

"Hmm," Miss Lacey said, unperturbed. "I know about Sam. Brilliant mind. I wouldn't wish to be him, though. Does that make sense to you? I suppose it's different, he being your brother. Only, Nellie, you may be better off. Sam will have a rough time day after day for many years, maybe forever."

"My Mama say he don't know when to stop talking! But she love him best, anyway, I knows that!"

"You think so? I doubt it. Different, maybe, the way he needs. Not best."

"Then why my Mama sending me and Jesse away?" Nellie stuffed a cookie in her mouth and waited for Miss Lacey's answer. None came. So Nellie had to go on. Her last words sounded awful hanging in the air.

"She really is. We going for the summer back to her home folks. Back to South Carolina. All the way back there. And we going without her—all by our own selves." And then Nellie added, "An' my birthday be in August, I gots to have it *not home!*"

"Where's Sam going to be?"

"Away at a camp somewheres, I don't know."

"Then what's the fuss all about? You're lucky to *have* a place to go to, can't you see that? The right place for you, not Sam. Away from a hot city—who knows what's going to happen this summer?" Miss Lacey brooded silently for a while, then she laughed. "I'll tell you a secret—I'm going to Chicago for the summer, to study. And I'll tell you something else. It gets mighty hot in Chicago in the summer! Even hotter than it does here. So, count your blessings, child. Why, you'll be having a *good* time!"

Nellie could see that Miss Lacey was only answering to say something, anything. There it was again—she really didn't care. Not the way Nellie wanted. It was like holding someone's hand crossing a street and finding, smack in the middle, they had let go to look in the other direction, not knowing that the cars were just whizzing past.

"They just getting me outa the way! All alone . . . s'poze something happens? Why, I could get buried in some old swamp down there and no one would even know!"

"Really?" Miss Lacey looked astonished.

"It could be," Nellie insisted stubbornly.

"Oh, things do happen," Miss Lacey agreed. "But you look to me like a young lady who can take good care of herself."

"Oh, if it was just me—but I gots Jesse to watch besides, and he never listen."

"Honey, I'm telling you something. You will have a good time. Better than cooped up here all summer! I can remember . . . do you want to hear? You see, I know what you are thinking, do you believe me? When I was a little girl, a very little girl, yes, smaller than you are, I was sent by train to my Momma—my own mother's mother—down in Mississippi. All the way from Illinois, down the Illinois Central line. Probably you don't know where it is . . . remind me, and I'll show you some day . . . but it seemed as far as death to me. We just traveled on and on and on. I was so sleepy . . . but I was afraid to sleep, afraid I'd miss my stop and just keep on riding forever. Grown-up people talked to me and shared their food with me, but all I could think of was that I would go on riding forever, right off the edge of the world, and no one would ever find me again."

Miss Lacey laughed a little. "It does seem foolish now, but I *know* how true it felt then! Finally, the conductor called out *Hillsdale*, and the porter helped me off with my little suitcase, and there I was. On the platform was a man in overalls, a tall, dark man, looking down at me.

No one else. Nothing else. And then the train pulled away. And, I tell you, Hillsdale was just *nowhere!* I wanted to run but I couldn't. That man came up to me, and he said, 'Anne Lacey?' and I just nodded. And he said, 'I'm your Grand-daddy Laird.' Of course I had known it, as soon as I stepped down from the train, but do you want to hear something, Nellie? I was ashamed of him. Yes, I was! My mother had told me he was a church deacon—he certainly talked like one!—and somehow I believed he would be dressed like the preachers in our church in Chicago, all in black with a fresh white shirt and a hat. And there was this man in *overalls!*

"Well, that was only the start. For when he took my suitcase and we went out of the waiting room, there was an old wagon waiting for us with two mules hitched to it! Not even horses, only those mules. You see, I was a proud little girl. I didn't know then that my Grand-daddy Laird was a proud man, too, but proud over things that mattered, not show things, as I was."

Miss Lacey shook her head. "Oh me, how I hated it at first! But by the end of the summer I didn't want to go back to Chicago. I cried to stay, and I cried when I had to go home again to our apartment, which was so hot, and the noise of cars and children, and the dirty smells of the city. I dreamed about Hillsdale every night until I went back the next summer, and then I waited for the summer every year. Now there's no one left in Hillsdale for me to go back to, but I guess I'll dream about it until

I die, even if I never go home there again."

While Nellie was listening, a strange thing happened to her. She stopped thinking about herself for a long time. It was almost as if she didn't even have a body to wriggle or feet that would fall asleep.

It had always seemed to her that everything other people said had to fit in with Nellie Cameron some way or another, either good or bad, mostly bad. But now Miss Lacey was talking about something separate. Her words came from the private center of her just as Nellie's words were a reaching out to others from her own hidden self.

She hated to think about the way she had stormed into this room after the Christmas vacation that made her sick. Why, she had no right to do that! Miss Lacey was a separate person, Sam was a separate person. Sometimes they met and sometimes they went away inside their own selves. It took a person to know a person. And that meant that Nellie was somebody, too.

Miss Lacey clapped her hands. "Well! Enough of that! Let's see what time we've got . . . five minutes. Want to try again? Why, Nellie! I don't believe I've ever seen such a big smile from you before!"

chapter 15

"A STORY TOLD BY NELLIE CAMERON
TO A TAPE RECORDER."

"I like the way that sounds," Nellie said. "On the TV
it say produced by and all that. Could we say produced
by Miss Lacey and directed by the author? Before I be-
gins the story, please."

"It's your story."

"Well, it is!" Nellie turned the machine on and spoke
as carefully as she could. "This story was produced by
Miss Lacey and directed by the author, Miss Nellie
Cameron, who be only in the third grade. Only," she
added again, for emphasis.

"This is a Fat Story," she said, "a story about fat

people. My Mama is fat. My sister Ramona is fat. My friend Emma Rice is fat. Some people say fat is no good. But *I* like fat people. Even Emma's paper doll Melendie is fat." Nellie switched the tape recorder off.

"Do you know something?" she asked Miss Lacey. "I never did think before how they was all fat an' nice. An' they is!" She turned the machine on again. "Only Miz Painter is thin an' she run around like a monkey, saying things I loves to hear but she making me tired moving so fast. Not Mama. Everyone say Ramona going to be like Mama. Emma don't say much neither, she just be there an' I likes that. Only Emma an' me not such friends since we be fighting."

Nellie took a deep breath. "That OK? Does it sound good? I been thinking about that since last week."

"That was a thinking kind of story, wasn't it?" Miss Lacey said. "Gave me something to think about, too. My mother is a little bit fat and . . ." Miss Lacey leaned close to whisper into Nellie's ear, "I sort of like fat myself!"

They shook hands on that. Then Nellie bounced out of the room, slamming the door behind her. In the girls' bathroom she met Doris Ames from the fifth grade and Lurana Vitter, who was in LaVerne's class. They were trying to light a cigarette and giggling so much they couldn't puff hard enough to get it going.

"Hey, here come Miss Goody-Goody!"

"Naw, that's not me. You gots to be wrong," Nellie said in a loud voice.

"Hey, lookit her! You sure she the same girl as before. You sure it ain't a spirit haunting her? Wowie!"

"Shut up!" Nellie said, loud again, and pushed past Lurana. "What can you do to me?"

Lurana could do plenty, let alone Doris, but by the time they had got over their surprise, Nellie had slammed out the door and was on the way back to her classroom.

Mrs. Grady looked up when she walked in and gave out with her usual sour smile. Then she waved Nellie up to her desk. "Just a minute there." She finished giving out the social studies assignment, then turned to Nellie. "Miss Lacey says to put you up to the middle group when you go into fourth grade, so I'm doing it. She seems to feel that you can keep up. In any case, the recommendation is signed by her, so she will be responsible. Remember that. Right there in her writing. I insisted on it. Not that I haven't worked my hair gray with you myself," she added, drawing herself up. "Still, something of Sam seems to be rubbing off on you."

The way she said that, softly and without her usual stiff anger, made Nellie see that it was a compliment, the very best her teacher could do. And with that, she was done with Mrs. Grady, smack polished and done.

Next year was a million months away, a whole South

Carolina away. She slumped down in her seat and smiled to the palm of her hand.

She could even keep her face to a nice smile, the kind Mama called "a storekeeper smile" which you put on when you went in to buy food and had to get it added to the bill, but you acted like you had enough money to pay that bill and plenty more—if only you wanted to but you didn't.

So she smiled at Mrs. Grady for letting her know about the promotion when school still had three weeks more to go.

She almost danced home from school, so full of her good news she thought it would spill out. She ran up the stairs, pulling Jesse after her. "C'mon, slowpoke. Why you always so slow? Why I have to be stuck picking you up all the time?"

"Aw, Nellie, please wait! Please!" Jesse began to cry as he puffed up the stairs.

"OK," Nellie said suddenly. "I'll wait. My, you slow!"

"But I ain't dumb," Jesse said. "Leastways I ain't dumb."

"I ain't dumb neither!" she flared up. "Don't you say that! I'll hit you. Understand?"

"Nellie, I didn't mean nothing. Don't you hit me! That Miz Harris, she in some bad mood today, she kept hitting an' hitting. She tell me I talk too much when she

watching her TV show, an' Nellie, I wasn't saying nothing only could I go out. An' wham! she whup me."

Nellie looked closely at her little brother. "OK, Jesse.
Only one thing, don't tell Mama. Right? That just our
secret."

"I can tell Sam, too, right? An' Grace."

"OK. Only not Ramona neither."

Then he was happier.

Mrs. Dempster opened her door. "I *heard* you
chil'rens," she shouted down from the top floor. "Come
on up, why don't you? I b'lieve I could find some doughnuts up here for you."

As they walked up the steep staircase, they could see
her tiny gray head peeping over the railing. "Hi there,
you Jesse! Hi, Nellie! Made 'em myself. Used to be the
best cook in Alexandria, is a fact. Come on in!"

She bustled past them into her tiny apartment. There
was a good smell of frying doughnuts. "My little friends
get first pick. He'p yourself."

They settled down with doughnuts and milk. "What's
going on with you?" Mrs. Dempster asked. "Been so
long since I was young, I don't know what you chil'rens
does in school. Never had much schooling myself.
About two-three years in all, I'd say."

"When I gets bigger, I'm going to Nellie's school!"
Jesse said proudly.

"Bless you, you are, aren't you? You look a right
smart boy, anyways. Your sister here, I bet she a big he'p

to you, like she is to me when I need her. Hey, Nellie, what you do all day?"

"Reading," Nellie said, "and we gots 'rithmetic an' history an' science an' art sometimes an' gym . . ."

"You don't say? My goodness!" Mrs. Dempster said admiringly. "That I'd live to see such a thing! You work hard now and don't miss out. Imagine . . . ! Here, have some more doughnuts."

They chewed away happily. Mrs. Dempster smiled at them. "You, Jesse, what's in your day now?"

"I got beat," Jesse said. "On my butt. That sitter lady, she real mean today, she say I be talking too much."

"Jesse!"

"You didn't say not to tell Miz Dempster, Nell, did you? It's OK to tell her, ain't it? I won't tell Mama, honest."

Mrs. Dempster said, "You don't look like a bad boy to get beat."

"I'm a good boy! Right, Nellie, right?"

"You OK. Sometimes."

"What a shame!" Mrs. Dempster said. "Well, I'm right glad to have you up for a treat, then. Listen . . . I got something else to do take your mind off your troubles. You wait right here."

When she came back she was carrying a deep brown guitar large enough to cover her from neck to waist. She held it lightly but with care, and her hands were at home on the frets.

"I didn't know you had something like that, Miz Dempster," Nellie said. "You play for real?"

"This is the onliest thing I do have, I mean something that really counts. This here's a Martin guitar, the best in the world. My husband played a fine guitar, that man, a fine guitar. Sometimes he'd pick up a little extra money playing here and there, but there wasn't no money in that kind of music, most everyone could play a little, so why pay good money out to hire a man? Stands to reason. My husband never would sell this Martin guitar, though, no matter what. So's I keep it, too, like it got a piece of him in it and a beautiful tone besides and I plays a little now and again."

She listened and tuned slowly and carefully. Then she played a chord. And another.

"Sure sounds fine to me," Nellie said.

Mrs. Dempster straightened up, smiling, then beckoned for silence. She began to sing to the guitar's music, eyes closed and mouth open. She sang, "Just a closer walk with Thee, Grant it, Jesus, if you please," and she didn't shout at the end, she only sang more and more quietly until her voice drifted away on one pure held note. Her face was entirely changed all the while she was singing.

Nellie and Jesse sat without moving. They held half-eaten doughnuts in their hands and forgot the glasses of milk on the table. They kept their eyes right on that old face, watching the wrinkles drop away from it as Mrs.

Dempster sang.

When the song was over, Mrs. Dempster opened her eyes and smiled at them. The sudden change was startling. "What do you think? Tell me another song, I'll sing it for you."

" 'Shake Sugaree,' " Nellie said promptly.

"You like that old song? My, my!"

"Oh, yes'm."

the time, then swung into it with her thin high old voice. Nellie sang softly along with her.

> *O Lordy me,*
> *Didn't I shake sugaree,*
> *Everything I got is done in pawn.*
> *Pawned my watch, Pawned my chain,*
> *Pawned everything that was in my name.*
> *O Lordy me,*
> *Didn't I shake sugaree,*
> *Everything I got is done in pawn. . . .*

There was no other sound in the room, there was no other sound in the whole world, it seemed, but the guitar and that song.

Then they heard another sound. Someone was coming up the stairs.

"Good thing I heard you up here," Sam said, standing in the doorway. "They'll go crazy down there looking for you. Why don't you tell someone where you two are going?" Sam grumbled on and on.

Nellie didn't hear him at all. She was so busy looking at his face she had no time left for anything else. And what she saw on his face was how unhappy Sam was. But why? He complained about things, of course. Maybe she just had never looked so closely before. His whole face was nothing but unhappy.

Why? She asked herself that again. At the same time she was thanking Mrs. Dempster and saying that, yes, she would come back and right soon, and she loved every minute of the music, and if she had only known before! And she wanted to go back right away that very night and listen again.

But Sam hurried them downstairs, rough and angry. "You're no better than the rest of them," he whispered fiercely, "listening to that kind of music. Wanting it! Where's it going to take you? To live like Mrs. Dempster, that's where! You want that? You're like Mama and where's she got to?"

Sam's being so unhappy somehow had to do with the rest of them being just the way they were. But what was that? Nellie wanted to be like Mama. Didn't Sam love Mama? He did! Of course, he did. He was always doing things for her. What was the matter then?

She worried about it so much at dinner that she didn't talk at all. She forgot altogether about telling her good news. She kept eating and looking at Sam. His face *had* changed, since he had gotten word about the summer camp and that school. He was at the table with them like always, but it seemed like only a mask of Sam, not the real Sam, who had gone someplace else.

After dinner she did something very unlike her. Pretending that she needed help with her homework, she tapped on Sam's door. He had a room almost to himself; Jesse slept with him but Mama put Jesse to sleep in her bed, then moved him in after Sam was finished with his homework and reading. That seemed right to all of them; Sam needed the room and the closed door. And he did not like interruptions.

Nevertheless, Nellie went to see him. She stood in the tiny dark hall outside his room for a long time before she tapped on the door. Then, without waiting for an answer, she opened the door a little and walked in. The room was barely larger than the three-quarter bed where Sam and Jesse slept. The only other furniture was a metal clothes closet behind the door and Sam's desk and chair. Sam had bought it himself last summer at the Goodwill store, sanded it, then refinished it, working slowly and with great absorption day after day until it was finished, and the golden oak surface was smooth to the fingertips and shone with varnish. Nobody else could touch that desk.

Sam was working in the yellow light cast by a heavy desk lamp, a gift from Mrs. Parton, his fifth-grade teacher. Nellie could see the dark outline of his profile against the light, and even that outline looked unhappy. She was truly afraid to talk to him, but when Sam turned to face her, he did not look angry, only tired, and his voice was very low. "What is it? What do you want? Can I help you with something?"

Nellie advanced toward him, holding her books out. "Yes. No. Oh, Sam, I wish I knew things like you!"

"No," he said slowly, "no you don't. Don't say that. Sometimes I wish I didn't know anything at all. Or only a little, just enough to get by with. Then . . . well, what do you want?"

"What was the matter with that music? It don't seem wrong to me the way Miz Dempster sing. Ain't she *good*, Sam?"

Sam shook his head. "Nothing's the matter with it. It's just that that religion stuff . . ." He looked up at Nellie's confused face. "Oh, never mind, Nellie. Don't listen to me. I shouldn't have said anything. The music's OK. And Mrs. Dempster's a nice lady. Want to see my work?"

Nellie leaned over into the circle of light. The book was thick, double-columned. The words blurred and danced in front of her eyes. Even the photograph slid away from her. "What's this? What *is* it?"

Sam laughed. "It's a special history book. I'm writing an essay. Not for class, nothing like that. It's for an American Legion prize. If I win, I'll get fifty dollars and

I won't have to ask for money when I go away this summer."

"You don't have to go," Nellie said, half whispering.

"That's where you wrong. I don't *want* to but I do *have* to. There isn't any other way. But I'd sure like the money. So here I am. Heroes of Liberty. Huh! That's the subject. Do you know what I'm talking about?"

Nellie knew, a little. "Sam . . ."

"Yeah?"

"Leroy, he say you said I'm dumb!"

Sam looked down. "That Leroy! Well, I'm sorry, Nell . . ."

"It's OK. I mean, I can read now. Really. An' I going to be promoted. Miz Grady said so."

"Hey! Good for you! Bet that make Mama happy."

"Oh, Sam, I didn't get to tell Mama! I forgot. I guess I *am* dumb. I kept waiting an' waiting to tell her since I learned—an' now I forget!"

Sam had gone back to his book. "Well, you told *me* and I'm glad to hear it. Really. Get to bed now, Nell. It's late. You can always tell Mama tomorrow."

chapter 16

Now TOMORROW WAS TODAY. Nellie woke up with a bounce and a song.

"Listen to her now, will you?" Grace teased. "And at this early hour besides. What's got into you?"

"Nothing," Nellie sang, "nothing, nothing, nothing." She went higher on the scale each time. "I decided that I'm going to be a writer. When I grow up," she added hastily as Ramona burst into loud laughter and Grace smiled.

"You!" Ramona pointed. "You tetched in your head? Mama going to have to get you prayed over next Wednesday meeting. What you going to write about?"

"You, for one thing! Ooooh, Ramona, I'm going to

"I wisht I could stay home."

"Me too! Me too!"

Mama was gone around the corner now. Nellie turned back to the room and slowly began putting the breakfast things away. The dishes went into the sink to soak until after school. There was a list of chores on the counter, same as usual: cooking for Ramona, shopping for Sam, cleaning for Grace, dishes for Nellie.

"Let's go," she said when Sam came looking for her. "School's be over soon anyway. Yippee!"

The day outside was gradually turning from the re-freshing light warmth of spring to the sweaty heat of summer. In the morning the air was still fresh and they all took in great gulps of it, knowing that by the time they came home from school, the leaves would stand motionless in the heavy heat and the sun would shine down upon them without mercy.

"Do you know something," Nellie said as she and Sam walked slowly into the schoolyard, "I hates the summer. I been thinking that I hated school so much I must be *loving* the summer, but I hates that even more. It just now came to me."

"Don't you learn in that Sunday school to love all that the Lord sends?" Sam asked, teasing her.

"I guess He must send my hate then, too, right?"

"Something's wrong with that argument, Nell, and you know it, too!"

She had no time to answer but she didn't mind. Sam

had talked to her in a different way, with no hint of his usual impatience in his voice.

Because Sam had been nice Nellie relaxed, expecting more good things. That was a mistake. That meant she was unprepared. Her own fault, really.

She went bouncing down after lunch full of words to spill out to Miss Lacey. It seemed that she was only now getting used to the idea of having this time for herself to use, and soon it would be over. Two more weeks to school. Then the summer in South Carolina. But she wasn't thinking about that yet. Only about her own lovely hour.

"Hello, Miss Lacey!" she sang. She seemed to be singing a lot of words these days.

Miss Lacey looked up from a pile of books and papers stacked on her desk. "Hi, honey." She was cleaning out an open desk drawer. The pile of papers and books on top of the desk was ready to topple over.

"Might as well get it over with." She turned to face Nellie, her face troubled and frowning. "Today's my last day here. They don't have enough money to pay me for June. Imagine that!"

Nellie was confused. "Money? I don't . . ."

Miss Lacey laughed bitterly. "Yes, money. I need my salary. That's all there is to it—I'm not one of those society ladies come and helps black children for *fun!* They told me when I took this job last fall that maybe the money would run out before the year ended, but since I started late, I figured they could stretch it out just for the last month. But there it is—not another penny. And why? Money for a war, yes, ma'am, why there's money for almost everything—if some important white person wants it, some congressman, some general—oh, as long as he's *white* and a *big shot!* I get so mad I can't stand it!"

She pounded her fist on the desk, upsetting the papers.

Nellie could only stand there, her eyes wide open in surprise.

"I thought things would be a little different, I really thought so, the more fool I was. So I'm off to Chicago tomorrow—can't even pay my rent without another check. My parents'll put me up until I get my summer school scholarship money in August. Damn! I wanted to get a little ahead, too." Miss Lacey sighed and turned her face away. "The worst is, I won't be coming back. No money for next year. What's a few dozen children who can read now when they couldn't in the fall? Nothing!"

She looked sharply at Nellie for the first time. "Cat got your tongue? Say something!"

Nellie shook her head. She felt very stupid. She should have expected something like this, should have known it was too good to last. All at once there came flooding over her the feelings she had had at the beginning: the shyness, the fearfulness, the failure.

Miss Lacey drew her close. "Guess I know what you're feeling. Me, too. Nellie, will you write to me? Do you promise? Write this summer, tell me what it's like in South Carolina."

"Oh, not me; I can't write good enough for you!"

"Just write anything the way you want to. Please!" She handed Nellie a slip of paper with her address on it in teacher-type printing. Then, before Nellie could say one word, she took a flat package from the pile on her desk and gave it to her.

"I thought you might like this—let me know what you think about it when you write to me. Agreed? Chin up—one thing you know now is that you don't need me anymore. Remember our bet? This," she tapped the package, "is my payment. Ooops! One more thing. Sorry—I almost forgot. Your book!"

Miss Lacey had made a new cover for it, with silver paper designs cut and pasted on red paper. In silver print she had written, *Stories and Poems by Nellie Cameron*, then the date. "It's all in there as far as I can tell."

"It's beautiful!" Nellie whispered. She looked from her book to the package, and back again. She dared not look at Miss Lacey's face.

"Keep it and look at it often—it's you in that book, and you thought you couldn't do it! No one can take *that* away from you."

They said their farewells quietly and sadly. Nellie was too numb to say much. Better to show nothing anyway —she had opened up and allowed herself to hope and now Miss Lacey was being taken away from her. Now there would be a new grade and hard work in the fall without anyone to depend on. Just when she was beginning to forget about the old scariness she had felt, here it was, flooding all over her again!

But once she walked out the door, she couldn't help wondering about the package. Miss Lacey hadn't forgotten their bet! She made a beeline for the girls' bathroom and tore open the wrappings. It was a large book with pages and pages of colored pictures. The cover had gold letters on a navy blue background. *Art*, it said, *for Boys and Girls*.

She hardly dared to touch the pages. First she put the book down very carefully on the floor and washed her hands at the sink. Then, imagine! Miss Lacey had put something on those clean new pages. She had printed in clear letters: "To Nellie, this key to open the door of one more room in a big world, from Anne Lacey to remember me by." Nellie did not quite understand every word, but they sounded grand and important.

Of course she would always remember Miss Lacey, with her nervous hands and her sharp, but gentle, voice. Oh, she missed her right now! The bell rang and Nellie tucked the book under her arm. Then she went back to her class, where no one paid any attention when she walked in, and she felt again the emptiness of no more Miss Lacey. She had won—and she had lost. Two more weeks of crummy school and no more hours in that beautiful blue room.

The only good thing was that she had her book and could really read it. She smiled at the blackboard, then wiped that smile off her face again quick, in case someone was looking. Then she yawned, surprising herself by her sudden tiredness. The heat made her neck damp.

All over the room feet were shuffling and sweeping the dirty wooden floor. Sun glittered in front of her eyes, a blaze of sun turning Mrs. Grady and the children in the front of the room to shiny dancing spots of light. In a few more hours she could go home with those two books, her own and the new one, and things would be just as she had planned, a circle of joy with herself smack in the center.

After everyone admired the book she would hide it in her private drawer, something for herself alone. Maybe she would take it to South Carolina, as a kind of luck charm.

Walking home slowly in the steamy sun, she imagined how it would be. She almost picked up Jesse, forgetting that it was Grace's day to come for him and pay the sitter. She was halfway up those steep steps before she remembered. "Dumb old me!" Her damp hand left marks on the book.

Soon they would all know! She walked a little faster. Sweat dripped down her legs. "I'm home, I'm home!"

She had only one foot in the door when Ramona was opening it. "Hi, Nell—here's a dollar. Hurry on down to the store to buy some hot dogs and a big can of beans, will you? There's nothing for supper." Grace was busy turning out the beds. She was singing "I'm getting sentimental over you" at the top of her voice. Scream, scream.

"Who does that Ramona think she is?" Nellie mumbled. She went down those steps bump-bump-bump from step to step. Long way down.

Seemed she stood in that grocery store line forever. On the way back she met LaVerne and Debby on the street, and they leaned up against a wall and talked.

LaVerne whispered, "Guess what? I really am going to Alabama, like I told you. Even before school lets out I'm going. Next week, in fact. You going to miss me?"

"You know I am. Last year Emma Rice done moved away on me. Now you."

"Yeah. Say, what you got?" LaVerne asked Debby, who had just come from the candy store.

"Nuts. You want some? Well, you can't have 'em. My Mama, she give the money to *me*."

"I'm going to Alabama. For good."

"Good riddance, you mean."

"*I'm* going to South Carolina, but only for the summer," Nellie put in.

"Too bad you not going for good, too. Might be some good things happen on this block without you two around. Country girls!" Debbie said.

"You talking!" LaVerne answered. "Where you going is all so great? Tell us that, eh?"

"You don't know what you be talking about, girl! Don't you know I gots me a sister living in Harlem? Don't you know even that one little fact? Well, I'm going to stay with her all summer for sure and maybe more than that. And I'm not talking about any *country*, girl, I'm talking about *Harlem!*"

Nellie spoke up. "My Mama, she say that where the devil make his home."

Debby looked down briefly. "Your Mama say that? *She* would!"

There was no room at all to introduce the story of her book, so Nellie said nothing more. The package grew heavy in her arms but still she stood leaning against the wall.

"Hey!" LaVerne suddenly said. "My sister'll kill me! I told her I'd be to her place by five to watch that Butchie. She gots to be at work! She'll kill me—I'm going!"

They walked over to the bus stop with LaVerne, leaning against the sign until a bus came and LaVerne snuck in the back door without paying. Giggling, she waved from the window.

"She gonna get her fool head cut off one day, leaning out like that," said Debby, stuffing her mouth with nuts.

"She don't care, not a bit."

"She be a crazy one," Debby agreed.

Nellie looked once more at Debby eating the nuts and went home. It was late and Ramona was good and mad! She was cooking rice and waiting for the beans and Jesse was in her way, of course.

"C'mere, Jesse," Nellie said, "I gots something to show you. In here." They sat down on the floor of the front room. She turned the pages of Miss Lacey's present as slowly as she could, just to look at the pictures and think. "See, Jesse, here's a house 'n some cows," and they traced the drawing with their fingers. Nellie couldn't make any sense of the long name at the bottom of the picture. Her joy sank through her shoes.

She turned another page and studied that name. "Hey, Nell, lookit this!" Jesse slapped his hand down and left a big jelly mark on the page!

Nellie slapped his hand hard. Jesse began to bawl. Nellie bawled, too. Her new book! Grace came charging in and without saying one word, slapped Nellie good and hard. Nellie cried harder and louder while Grace picked Jesse up and rocked him. It wasn't fair—he was the baby but he had been the bad one!

Silently, Nellie held out her book with the strawberry spot. "Why, honey," Grace said, "that'll wipe off." She did not even look at the beautiful page. The next minute the TV was on for Jesse, who was laughing with Grace at a cartoon show.

Ramona shooed Nellie out of the kitchen when she went in for the cloth to wipe it, and she teased Nellie for worrying over nothing but a book. "You losing your mind for sure, girl."

Nellie went back into the bedroom and crawled on

the lower bunk and just plain lay there. Nobody cared, no matter what they said. Not Mama, who called to say she would be late after all, as she was making food for a dinner party. Not Daddy who didn't come home because Thursday was a late shopping night and he made extra money if he stayed downtown.

The Ray Charles record they had bought way back last fall was playing good and loud and Ramona was singing along with it, lost in her own world. Grace was talking on the phone and Jesse still sitting in front of the TV. Sam was working in his room. There was no one at all to notice Nellie.

Then she remembered Emma Rice just as clear as if Emma were in the very room. The quiet comfort of Emma's low voice. The way Emma's eyes looked right into yours. Emma's slow smile. Nellie could see Emma's block right in front of her eyes. It wasn't so far. She remembered the houses spreading out more and some trees finding room for leaves and a little shade. Emma could not get enough of the Camerons, being an only child herself. She would share anything just to stay with Nellie. And she was plenty smart, she was. She would know what to say.

A longing like an ache came upon Nellie. She was astonished by the strength of it. Grace was off the phone and singing along with Ramona. Nellie went into Mama's room and found her old hiding place on the floor before she dialed Emma's number. It had been weeks since she had called Emma last.

"Hello," Emma's sleepy voice was the same as before. "How you *be*, Nell?"

"Listen, Emma, can I come on up now to make that visit?"

"Who bringing you on up?"

"No one."

Then Emma gave her directions. "Remember the way from the other time?"

Nellie wasn't sure, but she said, "Yes, I knows how. Don't you go out, Emma, I be there soon."

Moving quietly, she went to Mama's dresser and took five dimes from the stocking Mama kept hidden in one corner of the top drawer. She would have carfare and a bag of nuts besides.

With the TV and the phonograph both blaring, no one heard her leave. Once in the hall she could even smile.

chapter 17

‹›‹›‹›‹›‹›‹›‹›‹›‹›‹›‹›‹›‹›‹›

THE STREETS WERE JAMMED, buses rumbling, cars zooming, and noises coming from a dozen stores. Everyone was out in this golden hour, when the heat was leaving and a cool breeze slowly settling in. Why shouldn't she be out, too? The bus driver didn't look at her twice as she paid, which meant that he didn't think she was too young to be out alone. Now, if only she remembered just where to get off.

But when they went up the hill a little and turned a corner, she saw the big sign boasting Sea Island Style without any trouble. That was where Gran Rice worked as a cook. When it moved, she moved and Emma with her. There were just the two of them, Emma and Gran, and they went together with Marcus

Walker who owned the Sea Island Style and made the crabs and the fried fish while Gran concentrated on the ribs and chicken. Used to be Nellie could always get a tasty rib in the kitchen when she and Emma were playing with paper dolls or jacks, as long as they were quiet and did not make Gran Rice lose her steady hand.

"Got to keep it up for this child of mine," she would say, as she scurried in her cut-out slippers from the grill to the oven, never stopping, wiping her face with a paper towel. The barbecue shop had been hot and noisy but Nellie never minded, she was used to noise all the time.

She had been to Emma's new place only once, right after Emma had moved. Too bad their plans for getting together at Christmas had not worked out. And that fight! Yet Nellie was sure they were still friends. Some things did not stop. At least she hoped they didn't.

She walked slowly up the street, marveling at the big houses with porches and green lawns. The main avenue was almost as full of shops as her street, but the side streets had houses and grass and great overarching green trees that turned the roads into cool tunnels. Emma lived next door to the new Sea Island Style in a big white house made into many apartments. Hers was upstairs off the big porch in the front. There was another apartment upstairs in the back, three downstairs, and some rooms in the basement. Newspapers blew around the yard and paint was peeling off the wood, but Nellie still thought it was grand. The evening breeze made the trees swoop and swish.

She waited a long time for her knock to be answered, shifting from foot to foot and clutching her gift book. When Emma came to the door, Nellie saw she had been crying. The girls smiled shyly at each other.

"I been sick again," Emma said.

"I had the bus fare today," Nellie said. Neither of them said one single word about their fight over the telephone. Nor did Nellie ask why Emma was crying, nor Emma why Nellie was there all alone. There was no time for such questions which only made the other person lie in answer. They'd find out soon enough.

They walked down the long hall together, past the silent sitting room where they could not play because Gran kept her things just so, past the closed door of Gran's bedroom, into the blue-and-white kitchen with its clock ticking loudly in the silence, and the coffeepot set on the stove.

"You want some cake?" Emma asked. "My stomach's not so good, I can't eat anything." But she cut a thick slice for Nellie, poured some milk into a glass, and smiled as she sat down, her old sweet smile. They had to stay in the kitchen because Gran would allow no crumbs in *her* place, but the cake was fresh and soft, not half-hard like the leftover cakes Mama bought and heated up. Nellie kept on eating until she was full, all the while listening to Emma ask questions about the family, all about

Sam and Ramona and Grace and even that Jesse. She did not feel one bit bad about leaving them just like that without a word.

"Look at what he did!" Nellie said angrily, showing Emma the beautiful smudged book. "That old Jesse," she grumbled. "Why, they be so many in that house, no one even miss me if I stay with you."

Saying those words, she knew they were untrue. Emma shook her head and smiled once more. Emma was plump and light and quiet in everything she did, and Nellie admired her with the old feeling from last year.

Still, the quiet room began getting on her nerves and she had to notice how fast Emma tidied up those dishes, even if she was sick, before Gran had a chance to fuss. And she thought of Emma's crying and her being sick and alone. When Nellie got sick Mama would make Ramona stay home from school, and Ramona never cared, she hated school. She would show Nellie a dozen card tricks or teach her new songs or play jacks by the hour, and she could cook up custards or find a dime for ice cream or recite riddles until they both broke up giggling.

She told Emma a little about Miss Lacey and the beautiful book while Emma was swishing the dishes around in soapsuds, then drying them and folding the dishcloth just so, and Emma listened and nodded and worked.

Then she dried her hands carefully and came over to see the book, giving it her full attention. She read off the names of the painters smooth as milk, as if they meant something to her: *Homer*, she read, and *Eakin*s and *Sargent* and *Jacob Lawrence*, not stopping even at the hard sounds.

Nellie felt she would do anything, give up anything, to be so at home with these strange words, to make them move for her and turn themselves into a meaning. "Did you ever be happy and sad at the same time?" she asked, wonderingly.

Emma laughed briefly. "At times."

The long dusk of summer was slowly fading. Gradually a gray light settled on the room. Across the street, through the leafy trees, Nellie could see night coming on like a tired lady, creeping along, and reflections of lights snapped on in the stores. Barbecue smells came sizzling up and she was hungry. What were they doing at home now? "I got to go soon." She made no move.

"Umm." Emma was turning more pages in her careful way.

"Be nice if we could meet more," Nellie said, thinking that all would be the same between them then.

Emma smiled faintly and agreed. Between them was a kind of peace that made the room seem brighter. Who would look at such a book with this kind of care at home? Not even Mama. Sam, maybe. But Nellie did not want to think about Sam. She sat at the table as the night came on over the houses and right down into the dirty alley, and she felt outside of them all. Like Sam, she thought suddenly. Was this how Sam had felt? Nellie shivered a little and wiped her hot face.

"Getting sick, too? Gee, I hope not, Nell," Emma said kindly.

"Naw. Just tired." Why was she thinking about all of them? It made her stomach ache. She should have called home, she was old enough to know better. She could see them all wondering where she was, chasing around here and there. Lord knows, she had had warnings enough about those bad streets!

And then she felt good just as quickly as she had felt bad. They would all be worried about *her!* She smiled and hummed to herself.

Emma looked up. "My Gran says singing brings on her headache," she said, the corners of her mouth lighting up a little. "Not counting hymns, of course. *They* work wonders!"

"It does seem mighty quiet around here," Nellie admitted sadly.

"Oh, it is! Gran takes good care of me, though, that's a fact," Emma said with a sigh. "No one else do—not my Daddy, surely not he! Not like you, Nell, you lucky. So I be quiet, I guess. Gran work hard. And I, too."

Emma said this flatly, as if she had to say it but did not want to one single bit. Nellie knew that feeling all right and the same shrug of the shoulders that Mama gave.

That was the way it was. Not even reading would change that.

Miss Lacey acted as if reading could change everything. Nellie knew better! Take LaVerne. She could read OK. What difference did that make to her mean old mother? Would she sweeten up if LaVerne could read better? Not on your life!

Then there was Emma. Nellie looked up at her sitting on the other side of the kitchen table, one hand propped against her cheek, the other turning the pages of a book, studying. She was lost in some world of her own. Nellie could see that Emma was not happy. Before she had not noticed.

And Sam. Nellie remembered things he had said that night she had gone into his room, and underneath each word had been a drumbeat sounding "not happy, not happy." Yet Sam had so much, and he would soon have even more. It wasn't reading that made him happy or unhappy, it seemed. Anyway, Nellie would never be like Sam. She couldn't be. She didn't want to be.

What she wanted to be was herself, Nellie Cameron, who could read and who wasn't scared anymore. Well, not scared of most things. Just thinking of what she had done in coming here all alone made her stomach turn. And it was too late to call home now and *explain*. Nellie sighed. Would she ever get it! Mama and Daddy would fix *her* wagon.

She reached over to Emma's schoolbooks and took up

the one with the red cover just to have something to do. It was so dark that she had to turn the light on. Emma still sat, lost in her dream, moving farther and farther away each minute. Too late, too late, the clock ticked. Nellie sat still as still, only her hand moving to turn pages. She wanted to climb into the book and the pictures and never come out again. For once she liked all the silly smiles on everyone's face. *Your Friendly Neighbors*. A smiling nurse and a smiling policeman and a smiling doctor and a teacher fit to break up with laughing, and a milkman in a white hat giggling in his truck, and a baker and a grocer all plain delighted with themselves. Good thing none of her neighbors went around looking that silly.

The clock ticked on. "You feeling sick, Emma?"

"A little. Say, I'm glad you came this day."

"Surprise!"

They heard Gran moving slowly up the stairs. At the top she waited, then called, "Hey, you, Emma! You in there?"

"Yes, ma'am, and Nellie's here, too."

Breathing hard, Gran came in. Nellie knew that tired look well. Mama and Daddy always had it, like their faces would never stop hurting with all the smiles they put on it all day. Like your very breath and blood was coming out the soles of your aching feet. Gran gave her the smallest smile possible, then went on into the kitchen with a greasy bag. "Some ribs, Emma."

"I put the potatoes up, too."

Gran sighed. "Hey, Nellie, you staying? Help yourself. There's plenty. Thank the Lord for that, I do say, whatever."

There were no words to describe that food, its smell and taste. Crisp and black, covered with barbecue sauce, that meat was the best taste Nellie had ever had. She ate and ate, screwing up her bread to wipe the last of the sauce from her plate. Then she sucked her fingers. That morning, the school, Miss Lacey, her house, all seemed very long ago and far away.

Nothing like food to take away all the empty feelings. Even if only for a little while. Nellie remembered fights that went on and on when Mama and Daddy came home late and there was no food in the house and no money. Even potato chips and a Hershey bar helped then. But best of all were the days with chicken and ribs and greens and Mama's potatoes mashed with cream. Then you felt warm and happy inside and out.

Right now she felt almost warm and happy. Sleepy, too. But everything was not exactly right. Gran never said much but she looked sharp, not missing much. "What you going to do now, girl?"

Nellie started to cry. Very softly. Oh, she was tired! Tears came squeezing out on her cheek. "I better go wash up," she said and went into the bathroom. She was full of grease, so she soaped and soaped.

Emma knocked on the door. "Hey," she said softly.

Her low voice vibrated through the door. Nellie peeked out. Emma scuttled through the open door and plunked down on the tub side by side with Nellie.

"I got a fever," she said sadly, "and Gran says I got to go to bed. I been sick an awful lot. Something's the matter with my heart," she added, with an air of pride because she had a special illness. "Say, Nellie, come here again. OK? Gran says I can't go to see you. It's all the walking and stuff. You sure are lucky with that book and everything. I'm going to look for it when I get to the library next."

Nellie nodded. If she talked, she would cry again. Truth to tell, she was scared. And tired. Such a long day! She took a deep breath. "Maybe I could stay the night." But that was no good, they both knew. One more thing Gran had on the *no* side of her mouth.

She and Emma clung together. The visit had not started out this way at all. It was just the book and Nellie's pride in wanting to be able to blurt out her surprise. Be in the center for once and not just the middle. There was all the difference but she couldn't quite say it.

Still, thinking of the book and Miss Lacey, she did feel better and smiled a thin smile at Emma. "I be coming again. I promise."

And then Emma said good-bye and went down the hall to her room. Nellie listened to the soft click of her door closing, then turned slowly away.

Gran looked up as Nellie came into the kitchen. "Well, I called your parents an' your Daddy'll come and get you after a time. But they are not happy at your house a-tall, I can tell you, girl. You sure going to get it tonight!" she finished with satisfaction. "You got anything to run away from? Nice Mama and all! Sister Painter, she going to be dis-appointed in you!"

"I only wanted to see Emma," Nellie whispered.

Gran softened. "Well, that's right nice, child. Emma do need her friends. We lonely here by ourselves, that is the truth. Only next time you tell them where you be, hear?"

While Gran talked she took off her elastic stockings and heavy shoes. Then she sighed and leaned back in her chair. "Fetch me my basin of water now, girl."

Nellie knew what she wanted and filled the enamel basin from the hot kettle, then added some salts and a little cold water. Gran stuck her sore old feet in it and sighed again. After they soaked she would cut her corns and calluses. Mama did it, too, almost every night.

"Hand me my paper now." Gran unfolded the *News* and began reading, not to herself, but not out loud, either, just mumbling the words and making a little hissing sound in her mouth.

It *was* quiet and lonely. Not like at home. Even if no one cared about her book and her reading, they had things going on from morning to night. Here was only silence and tired Gran. The clock ticking. A light breeze sighing at the curtains.

Nellie turned over the pages of Emma's old schoolbook again. The pictures swam before her, then before she even knew what she was doing, she was reading word after word. The story began to make sense in her mind. All these happy people were running around because it was the girl's birthday. She would have a surprise. Naturally. Cake and ice cream. A lot of presents. And best of all—a puppy for her own. There he was in the basket with a big blue bow around his neck.

Nellie had always wanted a dog. They once had a cat to keep down the rats and mice, but never a dog. Mama talked a lot about the hound dogs in South Carolina. And Nellie would see one of them this summer.

Nellie blinked and looked at the puppy in the picture. *Jane's new dog*, it said.

A loud sound made her jump. Gran was pouring water down the sink. "You almost asleep, girl." She gave Nellie some milk to drink. "Your Daddy'll be coming right smart now, so you be ready, hear?"

Half-asleep, Nellie found her book from Miss Lacey and rubbed her hand once more over its shiny cover. She decided she would borrow Emma's old book, too, and finish reading about the dog. She would bring it back before leaving for South Carolina.

Gran was rushing her along, predicting a good beating all the while. Then Nellie could hear the sharp *honk honk* which meant that Daddy was waiting outside. No parking space, of course, with Sea Island Style still busy. Her heart jumped and she drew back but Gran almost thrust her out into the hall. Stumbling against the walls from tiredness, she went down the stairs on her heavy legs. Clump, thump. She sounded like an elephant. She giggled. Man, she was scared!

Outside rain was falling. It fell into the street lamps and turned yellow. The puddles on the sidewalk shone yellow and blue and red from the lights in store windows. The streets were jammed with people happy to be out after the heat of the day. A group of boys were chasing each other around parked cars. Music came streaming out from all over the street until it was completely around you and you had to dance. How far away was Emma's place all of a sudden!

This was Nellie's world and she liked it best of all. She stood for a minute breathing it all in. Then Daddy *honked* once more. Hard. She hopped in the cab mighty fast and leaned back against the cold leather seat. It was damp from the rain.

She waited for Daddy to start his mighty yelling. But he only turned around to give her one very long look before he put the car into gear and drove away, not even fast and angry but slowly, as if he were tired, too.

He had been talking to someone when she came down,

and he told her it was Pep Willsey, an old friend from Baltimore, and what a treat to see Pep after these four-five years and find out he was making it. Daddy shook his head. That was how it went. You never knew. And he had hit on the numbers today, too. Not much but something. So he had some good news of his own to spread around. Lucky for her!

It was as if Daddy didn't care about Nellie running off like that. Maybe after his meeting with Pep Willsey he understood about her suddenly needing Emma. Mama would take care of her, though, no doubt about *that!*

Meanwhile, Daddy was whistling as he drove through the packed streets, waving to friends and swinging around other cars. The windshield wipers went *thunk-thunk-slap; thunk-thunk-slap.* Nellie watched them, her eyes closing in rhythm, then jerked awake again.

Leaning forward, she watched as the rain fell easily, lightly, and washed the streets. Wherever there was a street sign under a lamp, she read it slowly and carefully, until she knew they were close to home.

chapter 18

◌⟩◌⟩◌⟩◌⟩◌⟩◌⟩◌⟩◌⟩◌⟩◌⟩◌⟩◌⟩◌⟩◌⟩

DADDY HURRIED HER OUT of the cab. The sharp impatience in his voice was one sign of how angry he was, coming out for the first time now that they were arriving at home. Nellie scrambled across the slippery seat, clutching her books and ducking her head. She slid out, splashing water all over her as she stepped into a stream of running water at the curb, and then she cried out. Daddy braked the cab hard. A line of cars behind them honked loudly.

"Now what is it?" Daddy called, turning around.

Nellie pointed. One of the books had fallen into the dirty water. Even as she watched, it sank a little lower and the soggy pages flattened out and floated.

"Well, pick it up, girl! I can't sit here all night. Got to get this cab to the garage."

Without warning tears came. Through their haze Nellie picked up the poor book and only then did she see that it wasn't her new book at all, but the old reader she had taken from Emma. They'd have to pay Emma for it, of course, but still . . . ! She rubbed her hand over the shiny paper cover of *her* book, wiping the rain off.

Daddy zipped away from the curb, and all the honking cars followed. Nellie just stood, exhausted, getting splashed and crying a little with relief and apprehension, holding Emma's wet and dirty book away from her with one hand, and clasping her book tightly in the other.

A car honked right next to her. Then she jumped! How wet she was! Running and stumbling, she went toward her door, which shone with light reflected from the street lamp through the rain. She caught her breath and sobbed once more, but by the time she dashed into the hall, she was finished with crying. She wiped her face with the back of her hand, letting the damp book fall to the hall floor.

At the top of the stairs Mama stood right outside the open apartment door. Looking up, Nellie saw her looming as big as a giant, her shadow even larger against the wall. Mama just stood there. She didn't say anything. Nellie walked up slowly, her feet feeling almost too heavy to lift.

"Well!" Mama breathed. Nellie looked straight up at her. Then she saw the tears running down Mama's cheeks. And Mama was just standing there with her hands at her sides, not wiping those tears away.

"Well!" Mama said again. She stepped aside from the door and let Nellie by. All the lights were on in every room. The first thing Nellie saw was the scared face of Jesse, half-asleep on the floor. Why wasn't he in bed? Ramona was slamming around the kitchen, making coffee and tea. In the living room Mrs. Painter was holding a Bible and biting her lip. They had been praying for her! Grace was leafing through a magazine, acting as if she didn't belong here at all, but she smiled a thin smile at Nellie, then went back to her magazine, every tense line in her legs showing exasperation.

"Oooooh, Mrs. Painter!" Nellie cried, and dove for Mrs. Painter's lap. She snuffled a little, hiding her face.

"What did I tell you, Sister Cameron? The Lord has delivered her."

"The Lord—and Gran Rice's good sense."

Nellie peeped up. Mama stood over her, larger than ever. Mama's big hands untangled her from Mrs. Painter's lap. Then Mama very carefully took the book from under her arm and led her past everyone in the front room and in the kitchen, right back into the big bedroom. Sam opened the door of his room as they went by and stood there silhouetted in the yellow light from his desk lamp. "You all right?"

Nellie nodded and Sam went back into his room. "Willie running around like crazy looking for you," Mama said through half-closed lips. She closed the bedroom door. "Come here, child, right on this bed."

Nellie lay down on her stomach, waiting. Her muscles tensed right down to her toes. She put her damp head down in the sheets and smelled Mama's sweet powder. What a good smell!

"Whom the Lord loves, He punishes," Mama said, drawing back. "Whom He loves." And Mama hit her good and hard, once, then twice, then once more for good measure. How those slaps stung! Yet it was funny how good Nellie felt all around those stings.

Mama waited. Nellie scrambled up, still smelling that good sweetness. Mama pulled her close and she snuggled against Mama's big warm self, breathing even more deeply of powder and hair cream. "Oh, Mama, was you praying over me?"

"Just what you think, child? We want to lose you? Or we wouldn't be scared? Oh, Lord!"

"I'm not deserving it," Nellie whispered.

Mama grinned. "Prob'ly not," she agreed, "but it say the Lord He love the sinner more than the saved and the one who returns more than the one who stayed at home. I guess that be true." Mama chuckled. "But don't you try that again, missy, never again, no matter what! Maybe the Lord keep His eye on you tonight, but He got an awful lot of looking to do right around the world, and next time maybe He be blinking at you!"

"Mama, I'm so tired! Mama, can I sleep in your bed like Jesse does? Just once, for tonight."

"First we gots to get some of that dirt off you, lamb."

Nellie kept going down, down into sleep. "Emma," she murmured, and smiled. Mama pulled off her clothes, then rubbed her face and hands with the washcloth. "Mama," she mumbled, "can I have some of your powder?" Her tongue was thick in her mouth.

"Honey, you been *bad*, remember? And wanting treats!" But while she was talking, Mama was sifting powder onto her chest and stomach, and rubbing it in with big warm hands.

Nellie made one final effort to open her eyes. "Mama, I been wanting to tell you for a long time—I can read now. Real books. Mama . . ."

She wanted to talk about her beautiful book which was in the living room instead of under her pillow, where it belonged. And Emma's poor book! Was it still in the hall? Inside her eyes she saw one of the pictures in her book, a yellow house on a yellow cobbled street . . . oh, she wanted to tell Mama about all of it! "Mama . . . my book . . ." And she couldn't say one word more.

Mama's voice came from far away. "Save it for tomorrow, child. This here's been a too long day, let me tell you. You not planning to run away again? Then it'll keep. I'm right glad about you reading—you know that, don't you? Course you do. Oh, baby! Go on, sleep now."

The very last thing Nellie felt before she sank deep into the sleep that had been waiting for her was Mama's kiss on her cheek.